Hidden Treasures of the Heart

Hidden Treasures of the Heart

Glenna Brickey Mayfield

ISBN: 0996245006
ISBN 13: 9780996245005
Library of Congress Control Number: 2015906520
Good Treasure Publishing, Riverview, FL

Philippians 4:13 "I can do all things through Yeshua (Jesus) who strengthens me."

New Kings James Bible

Matthew 19:26 Yeshua(Jesus) said, "With man this is impossible, but with God all things are possible."

Gateway Bible

Contents

Dedication

I dedicate this book to the following individuals:

To my Lord and Savior Yeshua (Jesus) who gave me the gift of writing and put this story in my heart. He gave me wisdom and strength to see this project completed. He proved to me that with God all things are possible! This book would never have become a reality without Him. I am eternally grateful to You my Lord.

To my loving and beautiful daughter Mika. You have been my number one supporter. Thank you for your amazing prayers, your continual encouragement, your love and your faith in me. You have been a jewel to stand with me to see this process completed. I love you dearly and beyond words!

In loving memory of two wonderfully amazing women who have had profound influences in my life and my writing and have changed me for the better.

To my Mother, Yvonne Brickey. You always gave me unconditional love and prayed for me daily. You never doubted my ability to write or that my books would one day be published. Your faith in me never failed. You were strong when I wasn't, and always had words of encouragement for me. Your prayers for me availed much! Your enthusiasm to see this book in print kept me moving forward. Thank you,

Mom, for standing with me, by me and believing in me. Thank you for being a wonderful and godly Mother, friend, counselor, advisor and role model. I love you and miss you.

To my precious and dearest friend, Betty Johnson. You were a constant encourager to me. Your words of inspiration sustained me, your excitement uplifted me and your prayers helped me stay focused on His ability within me. You provoked me to continue writing and you were diligent to pray for me. You kept me believing in myself and the gifts that God gave me. Thank you for being such an amazing and wonderful friend. I miss you!

Acknowledgements

SPECIAL THANKS TO Susan Eaves, my friend, coach and prayer warrior. You have been an amazing encourager to me throughout the publishing process. Your wisdom and advice has been priceless. Thank you for your love, prayers and generosity and for allowing the Lord to use you to bless me.

To my amazing daughter Mika for your understanding during the many late night hours and weekends of writing. You have never complained! Your constant help with research, computer work and the many prayers you prayed for me are priceless. Your patience and kindness throughout this process has been amazing! You've made it easy for me to fulfill God's will. You are truly an amazing daughter. I do "love you more".

Special thanks to my dear friend and sister in the Lord, Dr. Vernetta Williams for your help in editing, and your diligence in praying and encouraging me. You always kept me focused and pointed in a positive direction. You have been a great source for the help I needed and always so willing and generous to share your knowledge to help me.

To my many friends and family who have cheered me on during this process and been faithful to pray for me.

Thanks to Pastor Phil Derstine, Christian Retreat Family Church for your encouragement and conviction that my books would be in print! I am grateful that you are my pastor and friend.

I Peter 5:7 "Casting all your care upon the Lord for He cares for you."

King James Bible

I Peter 5:7 "Cast all your anxiety on Him because He cares for you."

New International Version

I Peter 5:7 "Throw all your anxieties upon Him, because He cares about you."

Complete Jewish Bible

CHAPTER 1

Dig Deeper

I PEERED OUT the plane window and stared at the endless sky and the wisps of clouds forming in the distance. As I looked at my reflection in the window, I noticed that my long, black hair looked a bit messy and that the natural, flowing curls that usually framed my face now seemed like a tight ball of yarn. My freshly starched white blouse was covered in wrinkles from trying to get comfortable. I was irritated with myself for wearing tan slacks when I noticed a purple spot from the spilled juice I had been drinking. I was grateful, however, that I was able to place my legs under my seat comfortably, unlike the woman next to me, whose long legs seemed to cause her intense irritation with every move she made.

My thoughts wandered home to Philadelphia and to my parents and my brother. I was born to a Messianic Jewish father, David Benjamin Jacobs, and a Brazilian Gentile mother, Alana Alexandria. I have one brother, Benjamin Aaron, two years younger than me. I love them dearly and will miss them terribly. I feel sad that I will be so far away from them and will not be able to see them for several months. Nevertheless, I know the time away will help me get some things into perspective about my life. I am still young, shapely, thin, and attractive, but also still single. It does not bother me very much to still be flying solo, but I just turned twenty-eight and not too far from the "big 3-0".

The thought of this assignment concerned me because I have had little training in Orthodox Jewish religious beliefs or customs.

My father adhered to many of the Jewish traditions taught from his childhood and incorporated them into his new faith. However, in our home, we never followed all the strict Jewish beliefs or rituals that I knew I would encounter alone here in Israel.

It was starting to concern me not so much that I was alone, because I was used to being alone. My concern was that I had not yet found my true purpose and destiny. I was excited about this trip because it was a new step forward in my career. I was thrilled about the new discoveries and uncharted territory that awaited me. I contemplated anxiously the long journey to my next assignment as an archeological photojournalist who specializes in excavation photography. It was a unique and special project unlike any I had ever had before.

I had been commissioned by the Israeli government and the Archeology Society of Israel. My job would be to photograph and document the findings of undisclosed and secret discoveries found in specified confidential areas. The sites I would be assigned to were under military surveillance at all times and clothed in secrecy.

I was certainly hopeful that there would be an ancient tomb or evidence of some palatial mansion discovered while I was here. Excavations south of the Temple Mount uncovered more than twenty mikvas (baths) of various sizes. An American archaeologist Ron Tappy discovered an alphabetic sequence in the foothills of Judea. The script was written on a stone that was placed in a wall where the alphabet would have been visible. The remains of a man in his twenties named Yehohanan (John) were discovered in Jerusalem. When the bones were examined, part of a rusty nail was found intact in the heel bone. This indicated this man had been crucified. I was excited to hear and read about all these past archaeological finds and hoped there would be some amazing discoveries found at my excavation sites as well.

I wanted to visit Mary's well and take lots of pictures for my dad. It is one of the most authentic sites in the Holy Land. It was the city's only water supply in those days. There could be no doubt that Jesus and his mother came here to draw water as the women and children of Nazareth had always done. The spring of the Virgin Mary is reputed to be located at the site where the Angel Gabriel appeared to Mary and announced that she would bear the Son of God - an event known as the Annunciation. I did some inquiry about the well and was told by another archaeologist that the spring gushes out of the mountain and runs through a conduit to a public fountain where women still draw water all day long! "How amazing is that?" I thought to myself.

Perhaps I would be as fortunate as the British Archeologist Sir Leonard Wooley who was best known for his excavations at Ur, ancient Mesopotamia. His work resulted in some dramatic discoveries, including royal tombs. He discovered the tombs of the first dynasty of Ur, which contained Queen Pu-Abi's jewelry, utensils, and other beautiful and valuable items. Oh, to find such gems, wouldn't that be magnificent!

I had learned only a week ago of excavations that led to the discovery of elegant long-necked glass bottles from Roman times, probably used for perfume. The bottles were under lock and key by the government, waiting for our team to evaluate and for me to photograph them. I could only hope there would be some hidden treasures beneath the earth's surface that had not yet been discovered, such as written tablets from kings or rulers of the land here in Israel. The finding, documenting, and photographing of such items would certainly bring even greater recognition to my work.

Little did I know, the greatest discoveries I would make would not be found in a mound of earthen clay. My discoveries would be secret treasures of the heart that had been hidden by my very own family. Secrets that had been locked away, buried deeper than any ancient vase. These secrets had remained hidden for many years beneath layers of pain, guilt, anger, and remorse.

The days and weeks to come would reveal mysteries of the past that I was unprepared to handle, and would bring me closer to my Jewish heritage than I was ready to embrace. These hidden secrets would change my life and the lives of my family forever. God had the key to unlock this well-sealed vault, unveil the treasure, and expose the secrets within. This key was me.

Luke 11:9 "So I say to you: Ask and it will be given to you; seek and you will find; knock and the door will be opened to you."

New International Version

Luke 11:9 "And so I tell you, keep on asking, and you will receive what you ask for. Keep on seeking, and you will find. Keep on knocking, and the door will be opened to you."

New Living Translation

CHAPTER 2

Special Blessings

THUNDEROUS CLAPPING AND shouts of joy filled the air as the 747 touched ground in Tel Aviv and our thirteen-hour flight ended. My weariness was replaced with excitement and jubilation as the plane glided across the runway to a gentle stop. All the passengers, including me, scrambled for their belongings with great anticipation as the cabin doors opened. I paused for a moment in the aisle to drink in the excitement on the passengers' faces, some just happy to be home again. As for me, it was my first visit to Israel, and I was ecstatic!

As I walked through customs and was quickly rushed through the check-in process, a strange feeling grabbed hold of me and took me by surprise. This place felt like home. "How odd," I thought to myself.

But before I could meditate further, I was immediately escorted to my car with a driver ready to take me to my hotel. I thoroughly enjoyed the twenty-five minute ride. I observed people along the way looking in shops or having a drink at one of the many outdoor cafes.

I had been given a large packet of information about the many places here in Israel of where to visit, tour and eat. I had jotted down some restaurants that looked really good! We had just passed Rothschild 12 Café on my list for best café during the day and a fun, happening place to be at night. It certainly looked crowded with lots of laughing and happy faces looking our way as we drove by! There were many outdoor cafes and restaurants on Ben Gurion Boulevard giving residents and tourist an opportunity to enjoy their famous coffee, cookies and sandwiches while enjoying the Tel Aviv weather. We passed Lethacamim Bakery, called the *best* bakery in Tel Aviv! It was known for its Challah bread and cheese nuggets. There was a line of people outside the bakery waiting to get in so I must remember to go back there! So many places to visit, I thought about my father and how great it would be if he were here with me. I felt certain many things had changed since he had left his country. I wished he could see the way it looked today. I thought how special it would be if we could sit together at one of these outdoor cafes, enjoying a cup of java, while engaging in conversation with the locals here. Oh well, it was a good thought!

When the driver pulled up to the hotel, I could hardly contain my excitement. This was the most magnificent hotel I had ever seen, much less stayed at, while on assignment. The Byzantine style architecture was spectacular with its tall, ornate columns framing the entrance. A walkway made of Jerusalem pink and white stone led to a beautifully marbled foyer. Several bust statues of what appeared to be Moses and King David lined the hall. Ornate planters and large crystal vases were filled with the most incredible white lilies, orchids, pink roses, and purple alstromeria—all placed by design throughout the lobby for the sheer purpose of enchanting guests' souls.

I soon noticed the strong smell of coffee along with the aroma of freshly baked cookies. Tables scattered around the lobby held elaborate platters of assorted delicacies that captured my eyes. I suddenly found myself at the front desk, a bit tongue-tied.

"Good evening, madam. I presume you're checking in?" inquired the well-manicured man in a stylish suit at the front desk.

"Yes."

"Your name, miss?"

"Sara Jacobs; Dr. Sara Rebecca Jacobs."

As the clerk looked for my name on the computer, I surveyed the grand environment with awe and delight.

"Dr. Jacobs, here is your key. Welcome. We hope you enjoy your stay at the Grand Royale. If there is anything you need, please do not hesitate to let us know."

"Thank you," I replied as I hurriedly made my way to the elevator.

When I opened the door to my room, I gasped with sheer delight. The room was not only spacious, but also quite elegant. The décor was earthy and warm. There was a large wooden bed, an inviting sofa, and two comfy chairs. All the furniture, including a beautifully carved desk, was handmade from the most beautiful olive wood. The workmanship was outstanding. A coffee urn sat on a table next to a platter of scrumptious looking pastries, along with a container of hot water and an assortment of teas. I drew open the drapes to my balcony. The view was absolutely breathtaking. There was a picturesque view of the Mediterranean Sea and the city all aglow with hundreds of lights flickering beneath a huge, yellow moon.

I slipped out of my shoes, and, like a child, dove into the middle of the magnificent bed. I sank into the layers of plush down bedding. It was warm! It was soft! It was oh sooo comfortable! I laughed and giggled, and laughed and giggled some more. "I could easily stay right here until morning," I thought to myself. "But no, I want to see more. I should go look at the bathroom."

"Oh my gosh! This bathroom is huge. And look at all these soaps and lotions," I thought. I picked up a bar. "Ahava soaps, how wonderful! Look at this." There were many different perfumes in a golden basket on the vanity. "This is magnificent!" I whispered to myself. I brushed my hand against the soft, white, elegant robe that hung on an ornate hook. An assortment of candies sat in flower-print ceramic bowls, the colors of blue, white, and gold. I was so happy, I couldn't stand it. I was told before I accepted this job that I would be protected at all times and well taken care of. I guessed this was the "well taken care of" part. Ooh la la!

On past assignments in other countries, I was always promised this type of treatment but never actually received it. The hotels were far from elegant—no ocean view, sometimes no view at all. There certainly were no toiletries, pastries, or plush robes awaiting me. I was quite surprised and impressed with the care given to me here, to say the least, and I planned on savoring every moment. This would be my home away from home while here in Israel. I would be escorted each day to the many different towns, cities and deserts where my work sites were located. The anticipation of when I could begin my work was increasing moment by moment. I could hardly wait to see what might be uncovered on these excavations. Little did I know the hidden treasure that lay ahead for me would be the greatest of my entire career.

I unpacked only what I needed for the following day and took a quick shower while inhaling the invigorating scent of lavender soap. I then toweled off and wrapped myself in the wonderfully soft robe. I ventured onto the balcony to bask in the aroma of the Mediterranean Sea and to enjoy the beauty of the moon over the tranquil city lights while enjoying a cup of Peppermint tea. I thought to myself, "How truly privileged and blessed I am. Life is good. Life is really good. Mmmm, life is so, sooo good."

I felt a peace here I had never felt or experienced anywhere else. This was very strange to me. I seldom had time to relax as I was doing now. My previous assignments left no time to sit and relax. I worked from early morning until late in the evening, going over photographs of the day or documentation that needed to be transcribed. I couldn't help but wonder what the working hours would be on this assignment. Would I have time to enjoy this balcony and the beautiful view and starlight as I was doing now once I got the call to work? I guess I would just have to wait and see. I had so many questions. I was always full of questions it seemed. Unfortunately many of my questions have yet to be answered. My dad always told me I was "too inquisitive" for my own good. I never did know what that meant and he never explained it to me.

I continued to think about my family, my career, my life, wondering what the future would hold for me. Where would my next assignment lead me? Would the accommodations be as nice as these? Would I have carte blanch in the next place as it appeared I would have here? So many questions and not enough answers!! I had to bring myself back to reality and stop my mind from running way ahead of me. I don't know why I was always thinking ahead on things that I really had no control over. I just needed to relax, take one day at a time, be patient and enjoy this beautiful place. I could feel myself getting sleepy and knew if I didn't move from the balcony I would soon be falling asleep right where I was.

Maybe I'd have just one more cup of this delicious Peppermint Tea. The smell was so enticing and its taste different from the peppermint in the States. I definitely wanted to shop for teas to take home with me. I know the fruits, vegetables and spices grown here are some of the finest in the world. Perhaps their tea and coffee is as well. Some of my colleagues told me not to come back without spices of Myrrh, Cinnamon, Cassia,, Saffron, Za'tar(said to be brain food) and Frankincense. Some of my friends use the spices with specific oils for medicinal purposes. They tell me they really do work! I wanted to find dates and figs to take back for my dad. He did tell me that once I tasted the figs and dates here I would never want them from anywhere else. I needed to begin making my list so I wouldn't forget any of the special items I wanted to take home.

The air was getting cooler and even though the breeze felt wonderful, I knew if I didn't move from this lounge chair, I might wake up here in the morning. That might not be the most comfortable sleep especially since I had an inviting bed waiting for me.

The ocean scent followed me back into the room and lingered with the scent of the freshly picked lilac, jasmine, mint and sage on my nightstand. I climbed into my majestic bed and slipped under the crisp, cool sheets, knowing I would have no trouble falling asleep tonight.

Isaiah 40:31 "But they that wait upon the Lord shall renew their strength; they shall mount up with wings as eagles; they shall run and not be weary; and they shall walk and not faint."

King James Version

Psalm 27:14 "Wait for the Lord; be strong and be brave and courageous. Yes, wait patiently for the Lord."

New International Version

Psalms 27:14 "Put your hope in Adonai, be strong, and let your heart take courage! Yes, put your hope in Adonai!

Complete Jewish Bible

CHAPTER 3

A New Day

I AWAKENED EARLY the next morning to the sound of bus horns echoing in the streets and sunlight streaming through the windows. I jumped out of bed, ready to prepare for my first day in Tel Aviv. After dressing in my new jeans, a soft pink tank T-shirt, and comfortable walking sandals, I hoisted my soft leather backpack onto my shoulders. I grabbed for one of my cameras before hurrying out the door for my first day of adventure.

I had to wait for additional documents to clear to begin my assignment. The paperwork and red tape seemed endless, but I knew it would all be worth it. I was told the newly requested materials were because of heightened security in the country and were for my safety, which I understood. I appreciated the concern for my welfare and accepted it as all part of the process. I thought everything had been taken care of before my arrival, but when I showed up, I found there was still much more to be done. I knew better than to argue with the authorities or the government!

I also had to wait for a call from the Archaeological Society representative at the American Embassy in order to begin my work, which could take weeks or even months. I was not informed of this new piece of information until I arrived in Israel. I was specifically instructed not to contact anyone, but to wait patiently until someone contacted me. The wait might be difficult, but I made it my resolution to thoroughly enjoy each new day by getting acquainted with the area, the language, and the people.

A New Day

I stepped outside the hotel into a gorgeous spring morning; the air was clear and crisp. The flower beds along the hotel grounds were vibrant colors of red, pink, and lavender. Everything looked so fresh. I stopped for a moment to listen to the wind with its gentle sounds and soft echoes as that of a lover whispering in my ear. The fronds of the palm trees were swaying in the breeze as if beckoning me into their embrace. I wanted to freeze this moment in my mind and frame it for future recall.

I had several places to see today, but my first stop would be the Western Wall, the most Holy Jewish site. It is in the midst of the Old City in Jerusalem and the western supporting wall of the Temple Mount which has remained intact since the destruction of the Second Jerusalem Temple (70 AD). I wanted to pay respect and homage to my father's heritage and to follow the customary tradition—placing a prayer in the wall's cracks. The Western Wall was visited by people all around the world as a vital center of prayer. When I arrived, I learned that there were separate places for men and women to pray.

I was already learning so much about the culture and people here. For Jews who reach out to the Western Wall, it is a window to a world of memories. They mourn the destroyed temple and yearn for its glorious past, but have returned to build their future in Jerusalem. I placed my prayer in a narrow crack of the wall, asking God to reveal my purpose and destiny and unveil the secrets of my family's past.

I couldn't help overhear a guide tell his group the Jerusalem's Old City walls built in the 16th Century have eight gates and all but one (the Gate of Mercy) still serve Jerusalemites as he called them and visitors streaming to its markets and sacred and historic sites. I was familiar with two gates, but not all eight. I remember my dad talking about the gates, but at the time I paid little attention because it didn't seem too important. Now I wished I had listened to him. I edged a little closer to the group so I could hear the guide describing each gate.

The Zion Gate is the gate of the Prophet David. The tomb of King David on adjacent Mount Zion was only a few steps away. The Zion Gate leads directly to the Armenian and Jewish quarters. The Dung Gate (that's the one I remembered hearing about because the name to me was so gross!). The guide told them this gate's unusual name was derived from the refuse dumped here in antiquity where the winds would carry the odor away (Nehemiah 2:13).

The Gate of Mercy is also called the Golden Gate or the Eastern Gate. This was the other gate I knew about. This gate has been blocked for centuries and is said to be awaiting a miraculous opening when the Messiah comes and the dead are resurrected. The guide conveniently left this part out of his description!

The Lion's Gate is named after two very scary and ferocious-looking animal carvings that border it on either side. I couldn't help but chuckle to myself because the lions are not lions, but tigers! This gate is also called St. Stephen's Gate, after the first Christian martyr. Some say Stephen was stoned outside this gate; others say the execution took place north of the city. This gate leads to the Pool of Bethesda, the Via Dolorosa and the markets. Herod's Gate had nothing at all to do with the Judean King. In Hebrew and Arabic this gate is called the Flowers Gate. The Damascus Gate is a busy thoroughfare to the markets. It was especially interesting for me to learn that below the 16 century gate, archaeologist have uncovered part of the entryway built by Emperor Hadrian in the second century AD.

The New Gate is the only Old City entryway not part of the original design out of the 16th century walls. The Jaffa Gate was the destination of Jewish and Christian pilgrims disembarking at the Jaffa port, which is where it gets its name! This gate still leads directly to the Jewish and Christian quarters and to the Tower of David Museum. This gate will also lead you to the most popular parts of the market!

I found myself sitting in front of the New Gate, looking at my own literature describing the gates. I was once again mesmerized by the architecture, the history behind each gate and the daily travels the people would have taken through these gates. There is so much to know and learn about this land. I felt more involved every day as I walked the streets and pathways to history. My heart was surely being drawn here in ways and for reasons I did not understand.

After visiting the Western Wall, I had an even stronger curiosity about this land, its people, and its culture. Perhaps it was because my father is Jewish and grew up here. Perhaps I was more interested in the Biblical aspects of this country than I allowed myself to admit. I decided that whatever the reason, I would make the most of my time here. I was determined to embrace each day as if it would be the day of my greatest archaeological find.

I headed back to Tel Aviv to visit Neve Tzedek and Neve Shalom, the first two Jewish neighborhoods outside the town of Jaffe. Both neighborhoods had narrow, winding streets, and were located not far from the sea, between the Carmel market and Jaffe. I found myself taking the time to enjoy all the sights and sounds around me, not wanting to miss even the smallest detail of life in this city.

As an archaeologist, excavation photographer and renowned photojournalist, I have traveled around the world to photograph, document, and write about priceless artifacts dating back to the first century. I've witnessed firsthand the unveiling of mysteries that surrounded these relics, but never had I felt the thrill I was now experiencing in exploring Israel. I was falling madly in love with this country. The many cities and towns I've visited captivated my heart and photographic dreams.

I felt a bit guilty for the complaining I had done over the years about not only the amount of travel I'd been asked to do, but also the lack of days off I had, and the holidays I had to work. My hard work and sacrifice had now landed me this prestigious job with scientists, archaeologists, and professors in the most controversial city in the world. Once my job began, I would be given governmental permission to travel in and around most excavation sites in Jerusalem.

These privileges were allowed because of the notoriety of my work done around the world in excavation photography.

By late afternoon, I found myself at the Garden of Gethsemane at the foot of the Mount of Olives, the place where Jesus and His disciples prayed the night before Jesus' crucifixion. I walked along in the shade of ancient, grand olive trees thinking about my father and how knowledgeable he was of scripture, both the Old and New Covenants. As young children we never understood why sadness seemed to dwell within my dad and on his face when he talked about "Yeshua," the Hebrew name for Jesus.

My dad could make scripture come alive with biblical stories he told my brother and me. The people in the Bible were so real and tangible to us it felt as if they came right off the pages into our home. I read many of the same stories, but they never had quite the same impact as when my dad told them to us. My father had an awesome respect for God's word. I had always remembered the story of David and Goliath and had now visited the very area this story had taken place.

Benjamin and I thought that sharing these stories and telling us about God's word would bring great joy to our dad. Instead, it seemed to bring a form of sadness or pain. As children we could not understand this, and as adults we learned to ignore it. There was something within me that knew there was a reason for my dad's sadness. It was as if there was a story he wanted to tell, but the pain of telling it was too difficult for him.

My mother, Alana, was the one who taught my brother Benjamin and me Bible verses when we were very young. She prayed with us every night and told us about Jesus. My mother was a "praying" woman. I had memories of seeing her by her bed on her knees talking to God with her hands raised in worship to Him. I never intruded on those times. They seemed so personal to her, but I often wondered what it must be like to have a conversation with God.

My dad would tell us about Yeshua, which was confusing for me as a child. I never understood who Jesus or Yeshua really was, or which one I was supposed to acknowledge. My friends used to tell me that I had the best of both worlds, as they put it, with both Gentile and Jewish parents. I didn't quite have the same excitement about it as they did. I was continually reminded of the sadness I saw in my dad every time he opened his Bible or talked about Yeshua. I couldn't comprehend how anyone could look so hurt or be in pain from reading the Bible. Of course, I did know that a Jewish believer acknowledging Yeshua was a complicated thing. It could result in excommunication from family, synagogue, or both.

I knew that my dad had accepted Yeshua after he came to the States, or so I was told. His parents had died when he was a young man of seventeen, so I was certain this hadn't affected his decision to convert. I asked my dad one time what he thought his parents would think or say if they knew he had accepted Yeshua. He got this strange look on his face. I thought he was going to cry, and then I thought he was going to be angry, but he just said, "Let's not talk about that, Sara," and I didn't pursue the subject with him further. In my heart I knew he missed his parents. I certainly missed not having grandparents on either side. I felt I had been cheated in many ways, even by God.

Before heading back to the hotel for the evening, I sat for a moment on a nearby bench and watched small birds fly in and out of the olive trees. Several perched on the ground in search of food. Back at the hotel, I took a shower and put on some soft, comfortable pajamas and a light, sheer robe. I was tired; more than tired. All my sightseeing for the day, coupled with the long flight, had given me double jet lag. I decided to order room service and eat dinner in. I sat on the balcony enjoying a wonderful hot kibbe soup, an out-of-this-world falafel stuffed with the most delicate lamb, and a delicious plate of hummus.

While enjoying a dessert of Israeli-style cheesecake made with Israel's famous white cheese and a delicious cup of hot coffee with whipped cream, I began to reminisce about the stories my mother used to tell my little brother and me. She told us wonderful stories of her parents, who had passed away before we were born. They were both killed in an automobile accident. My mom was an only child and she and her parents had been very close. She said she had never felt as alone as she did after their deaths. Mother told us wonderful stories about her parents. These stories made us laugh, and sometimes I would cry. It was sad to know I had missed the opportunity to know our grandparents and have them in our lives.

It made Benjamin and me feel angry at times that we didn't have childhood memories of grandparents like other kids. But through our mother's eyes, we fantasized about spending time with our grandparents and felt their love in our hearts. My mom had a special recipe for my grandmother's bread pudding. We used to make the pudding for every holiday dinner. Somehow this seemed to connect the three of us together in a simple but memorable way.

My dad's favorite recipe was a Jewish pastry called *hamantaschen*, which was served during Purim festival. It was a triangular pastry with varied fillings such as fig, pistachio, preserves, or hazelnut. Mom often used Dad's favorite—apricot. We loved making these delicacies, and it seemed to bring joy to Dad as well.

Unlike Mom, who told us great stories of her parents, Dad had never shared stories about his parents. All I knew was that they were both deceased. Each time I asked him any questions about them, he ignored the subject or told me he didn't want to talk about them. He told us he was young when his parents died. He said he had blocked the memory of that time out of his mind. It was too difficult to think about. He came to the States with some dear friends of his parents, since there were no other relatives to take him in.

Many times I longed to hear about my dad's life in Israel. I always hoped that he would teach me about God the same way he was taught. I hoped he would tell me what it was like to live in his country with all its wonderful history. Now, it seemed ironic that I would be getting a glimpse of what it might have been like to live here. Now that I was in Jerusalem, I couldn't imagine my dad not telling me about this place. How could he keep the beauty of his homeland, the people, and the memories a secret? Very strange indeed!

I spent the following weeks visiting many interesting sites. Hezekiah's tunnel was one of the really interesting sites. This tunnel was one of the earliest known archaeological sites investigated in the nineteenth century. I didn't walk through the tunnel because it is walking in knee to waist high water to get through it and I wasn't dressed appropriately to do that this day, but I knew for sure I'd be back to walk through it before I left Israel! From there I went to the Qumran, where the Dead Sea Scrolls were found. I later went to see the Shrine of the Book at the Israel Museum, where three of the scrolls are kept. The most prized exhibits at the Shrine were the two oldest copies of the book of Isaiah in existence. These Isaiah scrolls were a thousand years old! What an amazing exhibit to see. This small museum is an onion-top shaped building, designed to resemble the lids of the jars in which the Dead Sea Scrolls were discovered.

I visited the village of Ein Karem, not far from Jerusalem. It lies among hills surrounded by olive trees and vineyards and is claimed to be the birthplace of John the Baptist. I wanted to be on time to walk the Via Dolorosa, known as the "Way of Sorrows." Each Friday at 3:00pm a procession led by the Franciscan Fathers is conducted along the Via Dolorosa. This was the pathway Yeshua followed when he carried the cross from Pontius Pilate's judgment hall to Calvary, where he was crucified.

I went to the Pool of Bethesda, which was only a few yards from St. Stephen's Gate, inside the walls of Jerusalem. The pool was known to have five porticos. It was inspiring to see the discovery and remains of a fifth-century basilica. I saw scenes of country life reminiscent of biblical times. I saw many of the older generation Bethlehem women shopping for fruits, vegetables and cloth. I was amazed to see they still wear the traditional costume – a long black belted robe and a white veil flowing down to the shoulders. A string of coins attached to a red cone is worn on the head.

I saw a model of the city of Jerusalem of Herod's time which was amazing. Its construction took seven years of research, study and careful building. It occupies a quarter of an acre. The topography is an exact copy of Jerusalem during the time of Yeshua. The design and workmanship that went into restoring these beautiful places was certainly overwhelming to me as an archaeologist.

I was grateful to be here to hear the history behind the places I visited and actually see for myself the ruins and remains of so many of the areas talked about in the Bible. The stories mom and dad told Benjamin and me were truly imprinted in my heart and mind now and I felt I belonged here. I was truly overwhelmed by all I was hearing and witnessing. I had so much to share with my dad when I returned home.

I spent time in Jaffa, south of Tel Aviv. This was the city where Peter raised Tabitha to life (Acts 9:36). I listened to the guides tell us that this was where the cedar wood of Lebanon was unloaded for building Solomon's Temple. I was mesmerized with the history in this place. Old Joppa had become an "Art Centre," with great works of art, galleries, and jewelry shops.

The Mount of Beatitudes was absolutely my favorite of any site so far. The nuns were so kind and gracious, welcoming people as they walked through the gardens and gift shop. I wanted to find a quite spot on the grounds so I made my way to the corner of the Mount and sat on one of the rocks under a huge Olive Tree. I couldn't help but wonder if this could have been the area the crowds sat and listened to Yeshua give the Beatitudes (Matthew 5).

There are eight blessings in the Beatitudes, each a proverb-like proclamation. I could almost hear my mother's voice as she often recited the blessings to me and Benjamin. Blessed are the poor in Spirit....Blessed are those who mourn....Blessed are the meek....

Blessed are those who hunger and thirst...Blessed are the merciful....Blessed are the pure in heart....Blessed are the peacemakers.... Blessed are those who are persecuted because of righteousness. I wished my mother could be here with me now. I sat for a long time meditating on each one of these blessings and the teachings Yeshua gave about them. I felt so much peace. I would definitely come back here to enjoy the tranquility and beauty of this place.

I went to Megiddo, one place I *definitely* wanted to visit. I had heard my dad talk about Megiddo and he read to us that the Battle of Armageddon would be fought here (Revelations 16:16). I thought this must not be a very pretty place to see, but it was quite the opposite. It is an absolutely beautiful valley with lush green grass and fertile ground, nothing like I expected. I could hardly wait to tell my dad about this place!

I journeyed on to enjoy the brilliance of Solomon's magnificent structures. Excavations that had been done in this area revealed amazing discoveries of Solomon's stables, grain silos, and remains of houses and walls. It was said that an exquisite collection of ivory, one of the finest of its kind in the world, was found at the site. I was absolutely overwhelmed by the excavations and discoveries made here. I could have stayed for days in this one place. Each site I visited had its own unique structure and history. I looked forward to each new place with excited interest.

I thoroughly enjoyed hearing the guides tell about domestic life and items that have been found in the many excavations done here. There had been very little furniture found in the excavations. Some stone tablets were found in the more recent excavations in the old Jewish quarter at Jerusalem. Most of the houses we learned had flat roofs. The Jews loved to eat out in the open and would often have their meals on the roof top. That area was also used for storage.

Their cooking pots, pans and plates were mainly made of clay. Bread was the basic food. The wealthier ate wheat bread, but the poorer had to make do with barley. Bread was always broken, not cut. Now the scripture in Luke 14:15-24 made sense that says, "Let us break bread together". We were told that a wide variety of vegetables were grown here such as onions, beans, leeks, peppers and melons. Most gardens had fig trees. I was enjoying all the varieties of fruits and vegetables served here, especially the figs. I had never tasted figs as delicious as the ones here. I am learning much more than I ever anticipated on this trip and I wanted to absorb it all.

I listened closely as the guide told us about items discovered from excavations done in En Gedi, and Masada. Tunics, striped cloth, leather draw-string purse, a wooden powder box, glass perfume phial, mirror, jewel box, colored stones and a bone comb were some of the items he mentioned. This filled me with excitement and hope of what might be uncovered at the excavation sites I would be working, that is if I ever got a call to begin my work!

Proverbs 3:4-6 "Trust in the Lord with all your heart, and do not lean on your own understanding. In all your ways acknowledge Him, and He will make straight your paths."

King James Version

James 1:5 "If any of you lacks wisdom, let him ask God, who gives generously to all without reproach, and it will be given him."

New International Version

Proverbs 3:7-8 "Don't be conceited about your own wisdom; but fear Adonai, and turn from evil. This will bring health to your body and give strength to your bones."

Complete Jewish Bible

CHAPTER 4

My Guide

M Y DAYS OF exploration without any word from my employers turned into weeks and then months. It was now autumn and I've been in Israel four months. While strolling along the beautiful shores of Metzitzim Beach in northern Tel Aviv, I was beginning to really miss my parents, my brother, and my old friends, not to mention the familiar surroundings of home. I had met many interesting and wonderful people in Israel. But it wasn't the same as being around those I loved. I was feeling homesick. Also, I was told not to become too familiar with any civilians during my stay, which did not help matters much. I didn't like this requirement, but I also didn't want to be disrespectful to the authorities or make any decisions that would get me into trouble before starting work.

I began to consider how I had made major decisions in my life that were not the greatest for my career and had frustrated my father, to say the least. Little did I know there would be a major decision I would need to make in the following months that would be difficult and complex. It was a decision that would affect everyone in my family, especially my father. The decision, if not handled correctly, could cause incomprehensible damage to my family and my relationship with my father.

I had never liked making decisions that involved anyone but me. I made decisions that I thought would bring me happiness and success. There didn't seem to be any need for change, correction, or alteration in my life right now. In my mind's eye, my life was quite comfortable and happy. The plans I had orchestrated and designed for my life seemed to be working quite well! At least I thought so. However, I didn't realize that God had a plan for me that offered much more than I could imagine. His plan was for my good. I had often heard, "if you want to make God smile, tell him *your* plans." I guess I had made Him smile quite a bit, maybe even laugh!

The sky began to darken and storm clouds were gathering quickly while a light rain began to fall. As I briskly walked toward my hotel, more thoughts about my life consumed me. The focus of my life had always been on my abilities, recognition, and success. It was always about my work, my happiness, and what I could accomplish for myself. As I had traveled and made a name for myself, I believed life could only continue to get better. Yet, there had constantly been loneliness in my heart, a void I could not explain.

I found myself caught in heavy sheets of pouring rain, and my brisk walk turned into a fast run. Once in my hotel room, I shut the balcony doors and changed from my drenched clothes into the plush white robe. I sat on the bed listening to the thunder and watching flashes of lightening streak across the dark sky. The fact was, I missed my family terribly. This was an unusual emotion for me. I had become quite the independent working woman with a mind of her own. I had a purpose and a plan to fulfill that left no time for such sentiments.

In the late evening, tucked under the bed covers, my heart ached with emptiness that was too deep to speak of, even if there had been someone there to tell. I recited my usual prayers to God, asking Him for the Embassy to contact me. I fell asleep listening to the soft drizzle of rain as it dripped on my balcony. The next morning, just as the sun was rising over the beautiful Mediterranean, the phone rang. Finally, the call had come. I could begin my assignment. Thank goodness! It didn't dawn on me that my prayer had been answered.

Before I arrived in Israel I had been informed by the Embassy that I would have a local contact while on my assignment. His name was Jonathan. I was not given his last name, and when I asked for it I was promptly told, "Jonathan will be enough!" This contact would serve as my interpreter and guide. I couldn't help but wonder what "this Jonathan" would be like. Would he be pleasant, kind, considerate, helpful, smart and familiar with all the excavation sites, or would he be rude, impatient, no charm, no personality, all business, boring? I could hardly wait for our meeting, yet I was also a bit apprehensive.

Today I would finally meet Jonathan. I was so relieved to at last get the call to begin the work I had come here to do. I was to meet Jonathan within the hour to receive my first assignment. At this point, the only other information that the American Embassy would give me about Jonathan was that he was Jewish, lived in the Kidron Valley, was thirty-one years old, and single. While waiting for my call to work I had visited the Kidron Valley on one of my excursions. There is much Biblical history associated with this valley. It's located on the eastern edge of Jerusalem between the Temple Mount and the Mount of Olives. I read about King David crossing the Kidron Valley to escape his wicked son Absalom (2 Samuel 15:23-30). Yeshua had crossed the Kidron Valley to visit Lazarus to raise him from the dead. Yeshua also crossed this valley to go pray in the Garden of Gethsemane (John 18:1). It's a beautiful place to take a walk through the Archaeological Gardens.

I sat waiting in an open-air restaurant, listening to the splashes of water as it snapped against the seawall. I found myself listening to the many dialects in the conversations taking place around me. The aroma of Saint Peter's fish steeped in its array of spices filled the air and smelled delicious. At that moment it was difficult to believe this land had been torn by war time and time again, since there now seemed to be such peace. I wanted to photograph my surroundings, but I chose to take a mental photograph in order not to draw attention to myself or disturb the scene before me. I knew in my mind I would never be able to describe to my father, in a real and tangible way, all I had seen here and the impact it had on me. I only hoped

I could share from my heart, the joy I felt while I was here. It's certainly a place I will never forget.

In my moment of euphoria, I was startled by the abrupt sound of my name being called. "Dr. Jacobs…Dr. Jacobs." I turned to find myself looking into the face of the most beautiful man I had ever seen. To describe Jonathan as handsome would not be completely accurate. It was more than his looks that captured my attention. His eyes were etched with small, fine lines from the sun, giving him a look of ruggedness, yet his olive skin looked soft. His eyes were the clearest hazel I had ever seen. He was tall, with dark hair, and his build was that of a man who kept physically fit. He had a strong voice, indicating confidence, yet there was an elegant gentleness about him as he spoke.

"So pleased to finally meet you. I'm Jonathan." Any concerns I may have had about Jonathan suddenly vanished when he said "hello".

When he reached to shake my hand, I noticed his fingers were similar to my father's—long and slim, like the hands of a musician. My father played the piano, and I always enjoyed watching his fingers glide so beautifully along the keyboard.

"I'm sorry for being late," he blurted out. "But I had an emergency at one of the sites that needed my immediate attention. I hope I haven't kept you waiting too long."

"No, not at all." I tried to gain my composure, and hoped he hadn't noticed my surprised reaction to his stunning looks. "I've been enjoying this beautiful view. Please call me Sara."

"I detect an accent—Northeast?" Jonathan asked.

"Yes, Philadelphia." I smiled.

"You have been cleared by the government to begin working," he responded while handing me the necessary documentation. I've come to take you to the excavation site," he added.

"Yes, of course," I replied. "Are you also an excavation photographer, Jonathan?"

"No, I'm a scientist, geologist and archaeologist."

"May I ask why they have chosen you to be my contact and guide while in your country?"

"Why? You don't approve?" he asked.

"Yes, of course I do. I was just curious, I guess," I fumbled awkwardly.

"I understand," he said. "It's very simple. I speak five languages and know many dialects of our country. In addition, I am stationed at most of the same sites you will be working. It seemed a logical and cost-effective choice for my government to place me here. As a word of advice, though, don't ask too many questions," he gently warned after this explanation. His cell phone began ringing and he excused himself to take the call. While he was gone I nervously chewed on my straw, and fished around in my tall glass of iced tea for a floating mint leaf.

Jonathan returned a few moments later, apologizing. "Please excuse me, but I will be a bit longer. There seems to be some issue going on at one of the sites that needs my assistance."

"Take all the time you need," I graciously offered.

I looked out the window onto the open square and suddenly recalled how stubborn I had been as a child, always asking questions and wanting answers, even when there were none. It seemed I was doing the same as an adult. My thoughts once again wandered back to my family. I felt pulled between my dad's Jewish heritage and my mother's gentile upbringing. One day I was determined to have all my questions answered. I had no clue as to how that would be done, only that it would be. Now, I felt I was a little closer to having that desire become reality. At first I was apprehensive about being in this particular part of the world with so much unrest throughout the region, but now I felt more at ease.

I had also been concerned about the many dialects I would need to understand in order to work at the various excavation sites. Yet everyone I had met over the past few months had been extremely kind and patient with my pronunciations and wrong usage of their language. I had learned a great deal from the locals while on my travels, and with their help, I had improved greatly. However, I was still a bit apprehensive. I looked forward to getting to know the people on a more intimate level, and with Jonathan as my guide I envisioned this as a real possibility. My concerns were now calmed, and I felt certain I would have no communication issues with Jonathan helping me.

Ephesians 4:2 "Be completely humble and gentle, be patient; bearing with one another in love."

Open Bible

Proverbs 16:32 "Better a patient person than a warrior, one with self-control than one who takes a city."

Gateway Bible

Romans 15:5 "May God, the source of encouragement and patience, give you the same attitude among yourselves as the Messiah Yeshua had.

Complete Jewish Bible

Proverbs 16:32 "He who controls his temper is better than a war hero, he who rules his spirit better than he who captures a city."

Complete Jewish Bible

CHAPTER 5

Notable Day

I WATCHED AS Jonathan stood by the bar and continued his confidential phone conversation. I puckered my lips around the top of the tattered straw, taking a long sip of my tea while continuing to observe my surroundings.

Thoughts of how my dad had tried to discourage me more than once from making this trip came to mind. He told me it was because of all the unrest in the country. But I had been other places that were much more dangerous than here, and he never seemed as concerned. I remember telling him I loved him for being concerned about his "little girl," but that I would be just fine. My hope was that I could capture the heart of the people and the beauty of his homeland in my pictures. I wanted him to see how it looked today.

My dad told me many times to be careful and not to ask too many questions, which he knew I was prone to do. I didn't quite understand this, but agreed to be careful and use wisdom. I thought he was referring to questions about the artifacts I might see or perhaps even the site locations. However, I would discover these were not the questions he was referring to. I was still thinking about this when Jonathan returned, ready to leave the restaurant. He was quiet, hardly saying a word as we proceeded to the excavation site in his rugged jeep.

I wasn't sure whether to engage Jonathan in conversation and begin asking my many questions about his country, or to remain silent and observe for a while. My choice was to remain silent and wait for him to begin talking. I busied myself by taking in every aspect of the countryside and snapping quick pictures. It was difficult not to wonder what it was like to grow up here or to have migrated here from another country. I knew many of the locals did not totally value the historic or biblical heritage they had in their country. It reminded me of some Americans, who did not appreciate or comprehend the tremendous freedoms we had in our homeland. We seemed to take many things for granted, even people, as though what is with us now will always be there.

In the distance I could see a haze and knew we were getting close to the excavation site. The wind was blowing dust all around us. To dodge a tremendous rock in the road, the jeep swerved sharply, and before I knew it, I was almost in Jonathan's lap. He apologized for startling me, and I quickly recovered my composure. "Oh my gosh," I thought. "I hope Jonathan didn't notice my embarrassment about sliding across the seat."

There were many people working at the site. I knew from what I saw before me that this was a very guarded site. It was also a site where I would need to be precise and careful in my photographing. Everyone seemed to know why I was there, and they neither stopped their work nor looked in my direction as I got out of the jeep. They kept their attention on their digging and the sentry near them.

I quickly prepared my tripods and cameras, and began photographing the people while they worked. There were many reasons my work had gained notoriety as being the most precise in excavation photography. I was honored many times not only for photographing some amazing discoveries, but also for capturing expressions of surprise, delight, fear, and disappointment on the faces of the workers. Being an archaeologist added to the knowledge and proficiency of my work. I prided myself on the detail and expertise of my skills. Those who hired me expected perfection, only the best, and that is what I intended to give them. They would not be disappointed with my work, no one ever was!

I was known among my peers and with my colleagues as head-strong, willful, determined, free spirited, stubborn, and sometimes prideful and a perfectionist! I had heard these terms used about me many times, in most places I was assigned. However, until now, what my co-workers, colleagues or other archaeologist thought of me really didn't concern me. In my previous assignments when I had a job to do, I was determined to do it well, at any cost. It usually did cost me some friendships and relationships, but I learned to move on, in spite of the cost. I didn't feel that same way about this assignment or those I was assigned to work with. A very odd and unusual feeling indeed!

The sound of Jonathan's voice caught my attention. He was speaking very directly, almost sternly to a couple of the men in charge at this particular location. He seemed to be giving them specific orders in a rather harsh manner. There was now tension in the camp and a sudden hush had fallen upon the workers. I tried not to be seen as I observed expressions of fear on their faces. I later heard from the other workers that a small clay bowl had been unearthed but had not been handled properly by the workers. They told me something of that nature could be reason for dismissal.

What some of the workers didn't know is that pottery is no longer studied merely for dating purposes, but also to determine the types of clay used which can be traced to different points of origin. It's a very important discovery. The archaeologists were eager to determine: how this bowl was used, what it might have transported, and what information could be discovered from the area in which it was found. I was aware that containers will rarely be found with their contents intact, but the presence of residue offers a clue to what was inside. With improper handling, this valuable information could be destroyed. It was clear that Jonathan was rather harsh with everyone involved, but they all seemed to understand and were apologetic.

Even with the mistake of the workers, everyone was still excited that a piece of clay, an actual bowl was discovered. The archaeologists worked fervently to determine the function of the bowl uncovered— how it was used, what it had contained, and what could be revealed about the economy of the region. There was so much to learn about items discovered. It could be devastating for everyone if a worker did not go through the required process when a piece was unveiled. Fortunately there was no damage done to the bowl. I saw tremendous relief on the faces of the excavators and archaeologist when they realized the piece had not been broken. I noticed that Jonathan went to each worker speaking kindly to them. I sensed he was apologizing for his abruptness with them, even though I felt sure they knew he was only doing his job by protecting the artifact uncovered. He was reminding them of the way each relic must be handled. I have no doubt these workers will be extremely careful with every artifact unearthed in the future, no matter how large or small.

The sun was extremely hot. After a few hours in the desert sun my skin began to tingle from the burn. I didn't want to complain or stand under the provided tents. I knew if I did, I could not get the pictures I wanted. I had to move around the camp and stand most of the time. The dizziness I was feeling increased. The rays of the sun were at their most powerful and were burning through my clothing. It must have been more than 104 degrees. The man in charge insisted I drink more water and was polite and friendly to me. I decided to just sit on the sand with the excavators, hoping the change of position would ease the dizziness, which it did.

I was able to get some wonderful shots of the bowl that had been discovered and of the excavators and archaeologist working diligently and carefully to preserve the piece for further examination. I felt confident I had captured exactly what I needed and wanted to convey at this site. I couldn't resist taking a few shots of Jonathan as he busied himself helping to direct the men to where they were to dig. He seemed to have the respect of everyone there. It was obvious he had a great rapport with all the workmen.

Notable Day

There were moments when I noticed Jonathan looking at me. At first I thought he was just doing his job by keeping an eye on me, but then I realized his look seemed to be one of interest and intrigue. I looked his way and smiled, and he quickly turned away as a childish schoolboy would do.

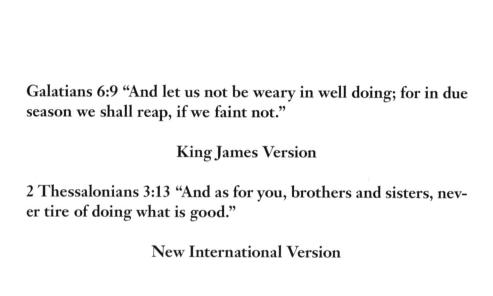

Galatians 6:9 "And let us not be weary in well doing; for in due season we shall reap, if we faint not."

King James Version

2 Thessalonians 3:13 "And as for you, brothers and sisters, never tire of doing what is good."

New International Version

CHAPTER 6

Small Finds

THE MEN AT our next site worked longer than usual. Each new day and each new site was exciting for me, even if discoveries of great magnitude weren't made. We moved to the area of Tel Motza, where many archaeological finds had been revealed. Motza was well known for its amazing discoveries. Our crew hoped that we, too, would make some tremendous breakthroughs in what was unearthed. The engineers, archaeologists, and surveyors wanted to continue working because they hoped to discover something greater, but exhaustion was taking its toll, and the light was fading.

Everyone agreed that the day's work had come to an end. There was a feeling of disappointment in the air, even from me, when we were told we had to pack up for the day. There had been moments of enthusiasm throughout the day when small discoveries were made. There had been pieces of ancient tools, broken pottery, figurines, and pieces of stone from structures, but I knew that we were all hoping for much more. I did feel it would come. We just were not digging in the right place. How true this would turn out to be for me in a very personal way.

As we were gathering our equipment to stop for the day, I heard a commotion among the men. I quickly asked Jonathan what was going on. He informed me that the archaeologists and engineers had found a very small vase in perfect condition. Its specific design, coloring, and graphics would enable them to identify the exact area from where this vase had originated, and the people who would have used the vase. I wondered if it was from a peasant village or maybe a king's palace.

I made my way closer for a better view. After the preliminary cleanings and documenting of the vase, I was able to then photograph and examine it. It was a small vase, perhaps six inches tall. It was beautiful, ornate, and turquoise in color. I presumed that it did not come from a peasant family, but from a place of prominence. I was able to capture the excitement of the excavators and archaeologists. I photographed them gently brushing dirt and sand from the crevices of this exquisite piece of history. The delight, joy, and passion for their work was evident in their expressions. The smiles on their faces as they looked at me said it all! I hoped their exuberance would be as exciting to my bosses when they saw the photographs.

I noticed Jonathan and one of the guards a few feet away talking quietly yet very intently and wondered what it was all about. I didn't dare interrupt, because it seemed more of a personal issue than anything to do with the dig. Jonathan handed the soldier some money and then touched his shoulder with a confident grasp as if to say that everything would be okay. The look on Jonathan's face was one of concern. I turned away so he would not see that I had been watching.

I decided on the way back to the hotel to inquire about the soldier and asked Jonathan if the man was all right.

"I have known the young man since my childhood. He is a man of character, honesty, and integrity—an excellent soldier," Jonathan replied as he looked straight ahead at the road. "He and his wife have two children, a boy and a girl. The boy is very ill. The soldier's salary is not enough to pay the high cost of the medical treatment his child needs. I give him money weekly so he can buy groceries and pay some of the medical bills," Jonathan added flatly, as if it were no big deal.

"That is quite honorable and compassionate of you. I'm impressed," I replied with admiration in my voice.

Jonathan dismissed my comment with a wave of his hand. I looked at him curiously. His face expressed a hint of frustration as the palm of his hand touched the center of his chest. "Where there is a genuine need in the life of a friend, relative, or even a coworker, I feel a responsibility to do all I possibly can to assist that person to make their burden lighter." Jonathan scratched the top of his head nervously. "Otherwise, life has no meaning," he added.

"I'm sure you are a tremendous blessing to your friend and his family," I replied again with an expression of sincere admiration.

Jonathan turned to me and smiled softly, "Yes, I'm sure it is a blessing for him, I agree. Thank you, Sara."

I had a thousand questions racing through my mind that I wanted to ask Jonathan, but I knew this wasn't the time to ask them. I was intrigued about his spiritual background from previous conversations we had. I hoped he would share more about himself in the days ahead as easily as he had talked about his friend with me. My own spirituality would soon be put to the test in ways I never thought, or even allowed myself to think about.

Jonathan's jeep moved smoothly up the lane, stopping in front of the hotel. The doorman immediately jumped off the curb to open my door. Jonathan leaned one arm on the wheel as he pulled his sunglasses off his eyes to the top of his forehead. "Have a lovely evening, Sara. I'll pick you up tomorrow at seven a.m. sharp. Get a good night's rest. I don't want you to be late and miss your ride."

"Don't worry; I won't. Thank you, Jonathan. Good night."

I anxiously ran inside and up to my room. I could hardly wait to take a shower and wash the sand and dust of the day from my perspiring skin and just relax.

Once I freshened up with a bath and a clean set of clothes, I ventured onto the balcony to relax with one of Israel's delicious cups of Jasmine Tea. The outdoor breeze was soft and soothing against my face. There was such peace and tranquility in watching the beauty of the sun setting. I was realizing with each passing day that my emotional attachment to this place became stronger and stronger, which I still found baffling and unusual. It was a feeling I did not understand or know how to explain. Perhaps it was the beauty and peace I felt among the Jewish people. I thought about my dad, and wished he could be here to share this experience with me.

I sat on the balcony for quite a while thinking about the day's events. I wondered if there were any relatives left here that I might be able to find and meet. I felt certain there was a story behind my dad's mysterious way of never talking about his parents or his life before leaving Jerusalem. Maybe this journey would prove to be more exciting than I had anticipated. I felt very tired and dragged myself into bed in order to avoid falling asleep on the balcony.

James 1:2-3 "Count it all joy, my brothers, when you meet trials of various kinds, for you know that the testing of your faith produces steadfastness."

King James Bible

Proverbs 17:22 "A merry heart doeth good like a medicine......"

NIV

I Thessalonians 5:16 "Rejoice always, pray continually, give thanks in all circumstances."

Open Bible

Proverbs 17:22 "A happy heart is good medicine, but low spirits sap one's strength."

Complete Jewish Bible

CHAPTER 7

The Confidant

THE NIGHT SEEMED much too short when my alarm sounded. I opened the drapes to find another gorgeous morning. I quickly showered, dressed, and hurried to breakfast. I loved the breakfast here. All the meals were wonderful, but breakfast was my favorite. The hotel provided a huge buffet with all kinds of delicious and nutritious cereals, fruits, yogurts, meats, fish, breads, and pastries of all kinds. My mainstay for the day, though, would be my water. Jonathan was careful not to buy water along the roadside for fear it might be contaminated. He kept a few cases of water in his jeep, which was gone by day's end.

I truly hoped today would be the day I would photograph the one tremendous artifact that would set my career ablaze. I hoped it would be something that would put my name in print as having photographed and published the greatest ancient treasure found in this part of the world. I would find a treasure, all right, but it wouldn't be one I would necessary want in print or have published for everyone to see.

Jonathan was waiting for me outside the hotel. He looked refreshed and handsome in his blue shirt and khaki pants. "Good morning!" he chimed in his Israeli accent. "We are going to a different site today."

"But why?" I replied, confused. "I don't understand. I have so much left to photograph at this location." I continued. We had been at this site for over a month, but I wasn't ready to leave. I felt there was more to discover there.

"Just follow my directions," he firmly insisted. "And don't ask too many questions," he warned again. I felt embarrassed.

"Don't be alarmed. It's a security issue, and has nothing to do with you," Jonathan consoled. I smiled with relief and settled in for the long ride.

There seemed to be no place in Israel that required little travel. I soon became glad for the long rides because it gave me time to get to know Jonathan a little better and to find out more about him. He was becoming quite the confidant for me, and it seemed very easy to trust him. This was a new experience for me, because I usually opened my private life to no one.

I had discovered the hard way that trust is not something everyone values. Some of my most personal thoughts had been exploited by people who I thought were my closest and dearest friends. This was the first time in many years I had trusted someone enough to share personal feelings and thoughts about myself and my family. Strangely, I found myself talking quite freely with Jonathan.

As we talked and continued on to the site, I couldn't help but notice the countryside. The view was exactly how my dad had described it to me when I pressured him for information about his home place. It was truly breathtaking. It was amazing to see the Bedouins lifestyle in the desert had changed little since the days of Abraham. Their dress was as it was 2000 years ago! Within their huge tents were mats for sleeping and tables made of round pieces of leather. There was nothing in their tents made of stone, and very little of wood or clay. Everything looked just as it did from archaeologist reports, drawings and photographs done by those working in these areas. I was absolutely astounded that this way of life still existed today and that people could actually be happy living like this. I wanted to photograph as much as possible and document every detail.

There were shepherds in the field herding their sheep. Caves where shepherds "kept watch over their flock" are still plentiful in the area east of Bethlehem. Children were running in the fields playing games and laughing. I thought of the children in the States and how bored they would be to play such games. It would be difficult for them to find things to do outdoors without television or computer games to keep them occupied.

Jonathan must have read my thoughts and said, "Interesting, isn't it?"

"What do you mean?" I asked.

"They all seem so content and happy just playing silly games, don't they?"

"Yes, they do," I agreed.

"Don't think it's like this everywhere here," he told me. "Children are not so different here than in other parts of the world. The privileged still have advantages over the less fortunate, just like in other societies. Kids whose parents are CEOs, presidents of companies, hotel chain owners, etcetera, all feel they have an advantage in some way because of their parents' status or who their parents are in the social hierarchy. Haven't you found this to be true in other places you have traveled?" he asked.

"Well, now that you mention it, I suppose I have, but it isn't fair."

"No, it isn't, but that's just the way it is," he replied.

"Jonathan, were you educated here?"

"I went to the University of Jerusalem for four years and then transferred to Switzerland."

"Why Switzerland?"

"There were several reasons. Switzerland was chosen for me. I wanted to pursue my doctorate in business after getting my doctorate in scientific/archeological studies. The International School of

Business in Lucerne is one of the best in the world, so my parents chose wisely. It was just far enough away." He sighed.

I could tell from his sigh that there was more he wasn't telling me. I hoped that as we became better friends I would learn why the decision to leave his homeland was made for him. I listened with intrigue as he continued his story. "I wanted to incorporate my two degrees so I would have trade options all over the world which would help fund new scientific studies," Jonathan added.

"Very wise," I responded.

"Thank you," he said, smiling. "And you? Where did you attend college?"

"I received my bachelor's at Columbia University in New York. It's highly appraised for the arts and photojournalism. Then I became interested in archaeological journalism and I transferred to Boston, where I was accepted into the master's program at Boston University for archaeological/biographical journalism. I also have a masters in archaeology. I later received my doctorate in archaeological screening with emphasis on curative photographical design," I stated proudly. "My goodness, you could go anywhere in the world and, open, own and operate your own museum." Jonathan chuckled.

"Yes, I could," I laughed.

"Now I understand why you were chosen for this assignment." He smiled. "I'm quite impressed, I must add. What was it about this assignment that made you want to come here?" he asked. It has to be more than wanting to sit in hot, dry deserts all day waiting for a piece of history that may or may not appear."

I thought carefully before answering him. "My background is Jewish, and I wanted to see where my dad came from. I figured I could accomplish several things at once," I told him.

"Like what?"

"Well, I wanted to travel and see this part of the world. I thought it would be a great opportunity to see where my dad was born and grew up. I am hoping for amazing archaeological discoveries while here so I can have my photographs and name in *National Geographic*, *Smithsonian Magazine*, and as many archaeological books as possible. I also wanted to do some 'digging' on my own while I make these discoveries, hoping to find my family roots."

"My, you surely are a determined young woman who knows what she wants," he enthusiastically replied.

"Yes, I am, and I most certainly do." I smiled broadly. "And you?" I asked.

"What else would you like to know?" Jonathan asked.

"Tell me about your family."

"Let's see…My father, Moshe, pronounced 'Moses,' is highly respected in his field and community, not only as a medical doctor, but also as a man of great wisdom and peace. He's now retired. He occasionally gives lectures in his spare time when not gardening or traveling with my mother, Rachael. The family is very close. My parents frequently visit my two brothers and me. They are always eager to hear what we three young men are doing or not doing, and if we are acting according to their wishes," he said with a smirk.

"My parents especially love spending time with Joshua, my Brother Joseph's five-year-old son. Mom and Dad have become doting grandparents with the birth of their one and only grandchild. As for my mother, she was always a homemaker. She has never worked outside the home. She does, however, do volunteer work at the hospital." There was a proud look on Jonathan's face as he talked about his mother. "My mother and I are very close," he added. "Sara, do you think there might be someone here who knew your dad's parents?" he asked.

"I don't know. There might be. My dad never talks about his family, and we never questioned him. I've often wondered if there could be a cousin or friend or someone still living here who knew my dad and his parents. I feel it would be very sad to leave Israel without ever trying to locate someone who knew them. My mother said my dad's parents were highly respected in their community and in the synagogue. She told me they owned a business here, but I have no idea what it was, or the name of it. I've asked my mother several questions about my grandparents, but like my dad, she's very private about my dad's parents and his life here," I told him.

"Is your mother Jewish?" Jonathan asked.

"Oh no. She's Gentile and Brazilian. She did live in Tel Aviv for a while, though. Her dad was an engineer and was transferred here from Brazil to work on some special project that required his expertise. My mom and dad met at Sacher Park here, and the rest, as they say, is history," I replied.

"History, eh?" He chuckled. "How would you like to have me help you in finding your roots?" Jonathan offered.

"Really? Would you help me, Jonathan?"

"Absolutely, Sara! I would love to."

Once at the new excavation site, I had to put away my excitement in order to focus on my work. The pictures I took that day were even better than the ones from the day before. I was well pleased with my work and never hesitated to voice it when the opportunity availed itself.

"You are a very proud young woman," Jonathan noted.

"If you mean I am proud of my work and accomplishments, the answer is yes," I told him.

"No," he said, "that isn't what I mean."

I thought to ignore his snide comment. But instead, I stored it away for a later hour after realizing that what he said had bothered me, more than I wanted to admit. Suddenly, I realized my lack of friends throughout my career was probably due to my determined assertiveness to get ahead. It was probably viewed as pride, even arrogance. I had never before had anyone confront me about it.

Isaiah 35:1-2 "The desert and the parched land will be glad; the wilderness will rejoice and blossom. It will bloom with abundant flowers and rejoice with joyful song..."

NIV

Matthew 6:28-29 "Learn from the way the lilies of the field grow. They do not toil or spin. But I tell you that not even Solomon in all his splendor was clothed like one of these.

Gateway Bible

Romans 12:2 "And do not be conformed to this world, but be transformed, changed, by the renewing of your mind, so that you may prove what the will of God is, that which is good and acceptable and perfect."

New American Standard Bible

Isaiah 35:1 "The desert and the dry land will be glad; the Aravah will rejoice and blossom like the lily. It will burst into flower, will rejoice with joy and singing, will be given the glory of the L'vanon, the splendor of Karmel and the Sharon."

Complete Jewish Bible

CHAPTER 8

Changes

SOMETHING SEEMED TO be changing within me that felt strange, yet comforting. Until this very moment, I would never have thought twice about the comment Jonathan made to me. Now, however, I was very much bothered by it. I didn't feel anger, which would have been a normal reaction for me. I felt sad that someone I was beginning to care about saw something that made him question my character. This definitely got my attention.

I would soon have a clear understanding of how pride had been instrumental in destroying valued relationships in my dad's life. Jonathan would help me realize how my own relationships were being affected in the same way my dad's had been. It appeared that God had me exactly where He wanted me to be in order to unveil His plan and purpose in my life. I sensed changes were taking place in me, but I didn't exactly know what they were. I later learned it was God's unconditional love and forgiveness working into the strands of my heart. It's so easy to run away or even excuse our ignorance when life becomes difficult. This appeared to be a pattern of mine that seemed to be changing abruptly and would soon change drastically.

Jonathan became such a good friend. He was instrumental in bridging the communication gap I had with the crew each day. He also helped me understand more of the culture and history of his people. We both seemed a bit surprised that we were developing a closer relationship. We didn't talk about it, but it just seemed to be budding like one of Israel's beautiful flowers.

One evening over dinner, Jonathan shared more about himself and his family with me. "I'm the oldest of the three brothers. Jesse, the youngest, is in college in America. Joseph, the middle brother, is Assistant to the Ambassador for International Affairs in Jerusalem. I'm the expert linguist in the family. I speak Hebrew, Greek, Russian, Arabic, and English. This has allowed me entry into several prestigious assignments over the years," he told me.

"I worked for a while at the Embassy and the Hebrew University. I gave lectures on the intricate aspects of being a scientist and geologist. I have worked alongside many dedicated and well-known archaeologists. I share with new and upcoming archaeologists the fine details of researching background, timeframe, etcetera, on historical treasures that are found. All this sounds pretty boring to most of my friends and they tease me a lot, but I just laugh it off. However there is something I do they think is pretty cool. I spend much of my time on a project with a local rabbi interpreting scripture from Hebrew to Russian for the Russian Jews arriving in the country," Jonathan explained.

Each time Jonathan and I talked, we became more and more at ease with one another. When I listened to Jonathon talk about his family and his passions, I felt my dad would really enjoying talking with him and getting to know him. I was certainly enjoying our moments together. At times he was very serious, especially when sharing about his work, but he had a sense of humor I had grown to enjoy and he had a way of making me laugh that I had not experienced before. I was really glad he had been assigned as my guide on these digs to find hidden treasure. I had no clue at this point in time of the treasure he would soon help me uncover.

Even though it was very difficult to work in the heat and dust, I savored and enjoyed each new day at the work site. I was not allowed to work continuously without a break from the job. Site officials set forth the conditions regarding my work schedules, and it was mandatory that I had breaks in between each assignment. This schedule had required a few days off for most of the sites I had worked, but somehow I sensed I would be having even more time off. The hours for the excavators had been extended above and beyond their required schedule, but it didn't mean I could work the same hours with them. I didn't like it, but I had to abide by the rules set forth on my behalf.

I thought at first more time off would be great. Now, however, I wasn't so sure. I was so involved with the excavations. I worked alongside these tremendously gifted and articulate excavators and archaeologists, making it difficult to think of taking a day off. However, it was out of my hands. I knew I must obey any regulations that had been set forth. I agreed to take the extra time off to rest. The temperatures were rising each day. I had to admit, it was extremely exhausting to work fifteen-to-sixteen-hour days in the dry heat without complaining or feeling the effects of it.

I took advantage of the days between digs to visit more historical sites where excavations had previously taken place. It was exciting to enjoy a bit of history while learning about architecture and biblical discoveries that had been made. I made my way to the Abbell Synagogue at the Hadassah University Medical Center. It held world-famous stained glass windows of Marc Chagall, each representing the twelve tribes of Israel. They were absolutely beautiful. The colors were magnificent. The light emanating from the windows bathed the synagogue in a special glow.

The research on these windows told me the Bible was Chagall's primary inspiration, particularly Jacob's blessings on his twelve sons and Moses's blessings on the twelve tribes. Each window was dominated by a specific color and contained a quotation from the individual blessings. I was in awe of the beauty and love I felt that went into the design and imagery of each window. Once again, my heart so wished that my dad could have been here to view this amazing beauty.

Of course, I had to visit the Jerusalem markets inside the city walls. I found beautiful tapestries for my mom and a gorgeous prayer shawl for my dad. My brother Benjamin loved jewelry, so I knew he would be most pleased with the chain necklace and matching bracelet I had inscribed with his name in Aramaic. I bought some Essence of Jerusalem perfume for myself. It had the most enchanting smell. I couldn't resist buying oils of Frankincense, Myrrh and Peppermint before continuing on for the day's excursion.

I decided to join another group on a tour through the desert which was always inspiring to me. There were so many different desert areas to see and the many flowers of all colors blooming here. The annual "latter rains" of March and April irrigate wheat and barley crops prior to harvest. Dry desert winds melt the snow and the desert becomes abundant with flowers. The crown daisy, rock rose, crown of thorns, snapdragons and corn parsley were all blooming and many more I could not name.

I was thrilled to get to see wildlife roaming the desert. The Gazelle, Ibex, and the Fire Salamander with its interesting colors of a black body with yellow and pink spots caused everyone to laugh. The most beautiful animal to me was the Sand Cat. It looks like a furry kitten. Its fur is a sandy brown with dark spots, some have dark stripes. We all passed quickly by the Middle East Tree Frog and the Marbled Polecat! I had no desire for an up close or personal view of these two wildlife!

I knew there would be more stops along the way and I took time to check my film and reload my camera. By day's end, I had captured some amazing footage of the barren, desert, and rocky places in the desert. The beautiful flowers and amazing wildlife pictures would certainly look great in magazines! This had been quite an accomplished day!

Romans 15:13 "May the God of hope fill you with all joy and peace in believing, so that by the power of the Holy Spirit you may abound in hope."

Open Bible

Galatians 5:22 "But the fruit of the Spirit is love, joy, peace, patience, kindness, goodness, faithfulness."

Complete Jewish Bible

CHAPTER 9

A Different Kind of Treasure Hunt

O N MY ARRIVAL at the dig the next day, I was informed that I would now have a week's leave, perhaps two. I had just had four days off! The seasonal rains were beginning to hinder digging at most sites. I was told I would be contacted when work could resume. Jonathan was full of conversation as he drove me back to the hotel. I didn't have much to say during our ride. I kept wondering what in the world I would do alone for a week, possibly two. I had already traveled by bus to many places of interest. Somehow, another bus tour didn't excite me. During the entire trip back to the hotel I was quiet and withdrawn.

"Are you ready for your new assignment?" Jonathan asked.

"New assignment?" I asked with a questioning look.

"Have you so quickly forgotten our talk about researching information on your grandparents?"

"No, I haven't forgotten. I'd love nothing more than to try and locate their burial site. It would be great to find someone who knew or remembered my dad."

"Then why the long face?" he replied as his fingers touched my chin.

"The idea seems really exciting to me, but I don't fancy attempting this endeavor alone and without transportation," I admitted.

"What makes you think you are going to have to go alone?" Jonathan said. "I'm going with you. We have the same days off. Don't you remember? I'm your guide." We both laughed. I began to babble like a giddy schoolgirl. Jonathan was enjoying my newfound enthusiasm and high spirits too much to notice my constant chatter.

My thoughts were darting in many directions. I couldn't help wondering where our search would begin. I had total confidence in Jonathan to take us to the right place for help. It would be awesome if I could tell my dad I paid our respects to my grandparents' burial place.

The idea that I might even find a distant relative who knew my dad or grandparents was more than I could comprehend. I just knew this was going to be a great adventure. My heart was racing with even the notion of it. I had no idea what treasures might be found.

Deuteronomy 1:29 "Then I said to you, Do not be terrified; do not be afraid...."

New International Version

Deuteronomy 1:29 "Then I said to you, Don't be shocked or afraid of them."

New Living Translation

Deuteronomy 1:29 I answered you, "Don't be fearful, don't be afraid of them. Adonai your God, who is going ahead of you, will fight on your behalf, just as he accomplished all those things for you in Egypt before your eyes...."

Complete Jewish Bible

CHAPTER 10

Shock Treatment

I GOT MYSELF ready to meet Jonathan for breakfast before we started out on our excursion. Since this kind of digging did not require bending over all day in the hot sun sifting through dirt, I slipped on a sundress. It was the color of cornflower. I let my hair hang loose around my face and shoulders. I slipped on a pair of delicate beige sandals and a straw hat with a matching beige ribbon. I used a light blush to bring color to my face and gloss to shimmer my lips. I liked what I saw. I guess I had forgotten what a difference a dress and long hair could make on a girl.

I took one last look in the mirror to adjust my hat, and noticed for the first time my striking resemblance to my mother. I had my dad's deep brown eyes and long fingers, but I had my mother's build and facial features. She was, as everyone said, very beautiful. Would Jonathan even recognize me?

Jonathan was already waiting for me in the lobby near the entrance when I strolled out of the elevator. The drastic shift in my appearance from khaki shorts and boots, with my hair piled under a hard hat was a delightful surprise to Jonathan. "My goodness, you look absolutely ravishing today, like a princess of the Nile."

"You like?"

"I like very much. Come let me show you off," he said as he took my hand and led us out of the hotel and into his shiny red sports car.

"Wow, nice car!"

"You like?" he asked, smiling.

"Very much."

After having a wonderful breakfast at a quaint outdoor café on Ben Ahuda Street, we strolled through several open-air markets to shop. Jonathan did a great deal of bargaining for me. When we came across a beautiful Star of David necklace, he bought it for me. "In memory of our time here," he said as he placed the necklace around my neck. We walked along the boardwalk and stopped to enjoy the view of the gorgeous Mediterranean Sea and admire its beautiful shade of deep blue and the crystal clearness of its waters. It was fun for me to see Jonathan more relaxed than his usual serious self I saw at work. He was quite talkative, very attentive, and we laughed a lot. These were wonderful memories I would not soon forget. Tourists were scurrying around with their cameras capturing their own memories.

By noon, our first stop was at the Office of Vital Statistics. Jonathan spoke their language and it seemed like everyone knew him and gave him whatever he asked for. Jonathan flipped through some papers the clerk had given him, and within a moment said, "I found the names of your dad's parents." Then his face fell into a concerned and pale expression.

"What's wrong?" I asked.

"Nothing, nothing," he said, as he continued to read the documents in his hand.

"Where are they buried? Does it say?" I asked.

Jonathan took my hands into his and looked into my eyes with deep compassion. "Sara, your grandparents are *not dead*, but very much *alive*. They live close by."

I felt dizzy and started to sway. Jonathan helped me to a bench and asked the clerk for some water.

"There must be some mistake. They can't be *alive*. That's not possible," I said, confused. "My father told us his parents were dead. That is why he emigrated to the States," I murmured.

"According to these documents, your grandparents are *very much alive*, Sara." Jonathan had such tender concern in his eyes. "Sara, I don't know what this is about, but we can end this now and not go any further. It may be best. If they are alive, there must be good reasons for your father keeping this from you."

"*Best?*" I screamed. "How could it be best? I have grandparents who are alive—living here in Jerusalem, where my father knew I was coming. He could have told me about them. Why, Jonathan? Why didn't he tell me about them?" I pleaded. "Why did he lie to us all these years? What could be so terrible that he buried them alive in his mind and heart?"

"I don't know, Sara, but your father must have had his reasons," Jonathan suggested.

"Yes, he must have, and I'd like to know what they are! Jonathan, I want to go see my grandparents. I need to see my grandparents," I insisted.

"Sara, what if they don't know about you? What if…I'm sorry, it is not my place to interfere. I will take you tomorrow to where they live. I believe it would be wise to take the rest of the night to think about how to approach meeting your grandparents and what you will say to them. Sara, consider how they may react to learning of you as well. We don't know how they will respond to you, Sara. We don't know what the relationship between your grandparents and your father was."

Jonathan's advice was helpful. I agreed to wait because I knew I needed some time to figure out what I'd say to them. I also needed the strength to face whatever would result from the encounter

What if Jonathan was right? What if they didn't know about me? Or worse, didn't want to know me? I slept very little that night. My mind was racing with thoughts of my childhood birthday parties, Christmases, school events, Hanukkahs and graduations—I wished my grandparents could have been there for those special times. I had a million questions for my dad, but my anger toward him wouldn't allow me to think about him right now.

John 14:27 "Peace I leave with you, My peace I give you; not as the world gives do I give to you. Let not your heart be troubled, neither let it be afraid."

New American Standard

John 16:33 "These things I have spoken to you, that in Me you may have peace. In the world ye shall have tribulation: but be of good cheer; I have overcome the world""

New American Standard

CHAPTER 11

Ready or Not

I GOT UP before dawn, and for the first time in many years I found myself praying. I prayed like I had as a little girl, on my knees, hands folded, in front of the majestic bed. I wasn't sure what to say, or even if God would listen to me. It wasn't like we had been on a first-name basis, at least I didn't think so. But as I would later discover, God knew my name very well. He knew everything about me, and strangest of all, He loved me just the way I was. This revelation was the most difficult to accept. I had been told from early childhood that Yeshua loved me, but because I had never personally experienced this love, I hadn't accepted this truth. Now I wondered how a God who loved me could keep grandparents from me whom I had longed for my entire life.

What could be so terrible for my dad to just *forget* his parents were here and alive? Or did he forget? Did my mom know? If she did, why did she keep it from me? I was so angry with my father for keeping this secret for over twenty-eight years. Why would he do such a thing? I pondered these thoughts and many more all day. I was irritated, agitated, and hurt. Jonathan called several times to check on me, but our conversations were short. I just didn't want to talk. I was embarrassed and wondered what he thought of this whole situation. But his kindness seemed to wash away any thoughts of embarrassment, which helped me to relax and think clearly. I slept very little again that night, wondering, "Am I ready for an encounter with my grandparents?"

The next morning I met Jonathan in the lobby wearing my Sunday best: a new pink dress, a jacket the color of soft lilac with a flower print, and dressy pump sandals. Jonathan's eyes said everything when he saw me. "You look beautiful."

"Thank you. I hope it's okay."

"It's more than okay. It's perfect. You look gorgeous."

The drive to my grandparent's home was only twenty minutes, but it felt more like hours to me. I could feel my heart pounding with every mile. Jonathan pulled his car to a halt in front of a beautiful, large, stone cottage. It looked like a picture from a magazine. There were flowers all around the portico and a flower bed on the side of the house. I wondered what my dad would say if he knew what I was about to do. Then I pushed the thought aside as anger once again rose within me to know he kept such an important part of his heritage from my brother and me. I thought of Benjamin and what he might say. This treasure was certainly different from any I had expected to find in Israel. It was not a treasure to keep hidden, or secretly tucked away in another part of the world.

My brother was always so easygoing and forgiving of everything and everyone. He would readily accept this news and have some excuse for our dad's behavior. I wished he could be with me now and that I could lean on him. He listened to my complaints, tolerated my moods, and loved me through it all. He accepted our dad's faith and incorporated our mother's as well. It seemed he felt he had the best of both worlds, and perhaps he did. I had just never determined which faith fit into my life or which one I wanted, the Jewish or the Christian faith.

Benjamin and my dad were very close, as it should be for father and son. They spent a lot of time doing things together. I guess my stubbornness kept my dad and me from becoming as close as he and Benjamin, but my mom always said I was just like my dad. Maybe now I could find out from his parents if that were really true.

I began to reminisce about the decisions I had made throughout my life. Sometimes I thought them through, and other times I just decided things on the spot. That usually didn't turn out too well. This time my heart would be very involved in the decisions I would make regarding the hidden treasure I had uncovered. My hope was that the decisions I made about this discovery would not destroy or damage my relationship with my father. I couldn't begin to fathom what he would say or do when I told him. I didn't want to think about that right now.

I was about to meet my grandparents for the first time. "Ready or not," I thought, here I come!"

I was anxious to hear what their son was like growing up, and what happened to cause such a separation between them. Would they tell me? Would they want to talk with me? Oh my goodness, my heart was racing.

"Are you ready?" Jonathan asked.

"Yes, I believe so...I hope so." I smiled nervously.

"Are you sure?" he asked again.

"Yes, I'm sure."

Philippians 4:6-7 "Be anxious for nothing, but in everything by prayer and supplication, with thanksgiving, let your request be made known to God; and the peace of God, which surpasses all understanding will guard your hearts and minds through Jesus.

New American Standard

Isaiah 41:10 "So do not fear; I am with you; do not be dismayed, for I am your God. I will strengthen you and help you. I will uphold you with my righteous right hand."

New American Standard

CHAPTER 12

Secrets Exposed

JONATHAN RAN TO join me as I walked ahead to the front door. "I will go with you. They may not speak English," he said. Jonathan knocked on the door gingerly. Perhaps he hoped they wouldn't hear the knock, and he could convince me to leave. I pounded loudly on the door a few more times.

A tall, distinguished-looking man with olive skin and salt-and-pepper hair opened the door. He greeted us in Hebrew. Jonathan responded back to the man in Hebrew, introducing himself. He showed his identification from the Hebrew University and Archeological Society. He introduced me simply as Sara. Jonathan asked if he was the Mr. Aaron Jacobs that we were told lived here.

"Yes, of course, what can I do for you?" the man replied in Hebrew.

"It is a delicate matter," Jonathan responded. May we come in for a moment? Do you speak English, Mr. Jacobs? My friend here is from America."

"Yes, yes, of course. We speak English. Welcome, Miss Sara. Please, please, come in," Mr. Jacobs insisted.

We entered the living room and sat down. I could tell from the beautiful furnishings, elegant wall coverings, and the many famous paintings on the walls that my grandfather had done quite well in the business world.

Pink roses cut from the outside garden were in delicately etched crystal vases on the dining table and end tables. "They have the same love for flowers as I do," I thought to myself. We all sat down in the living room, and then there was an awkward moment of silence.

"Can I get you anything to drink? Tea? Water?" asked Mr. Jacobs.

"Not right now. No thank you, Mr. Jacobs. Is Mrs. Jacobs home?" asked Jonathan.

At that moment, an attractive, petite woman who looked to be in her early sixties walked into the room. She brushed her hair away from her face and asked my grandfather in Hebrew, "Aaron, who are these people?" I knew this was my grandmother, because she had the same eyes as my dad and the same serious expression.

My grandfather looked at her with concern, "I don't know. They have something to discuss with us. They said it is very important. Come, sit," he said. My grandmother sat next to her husband, and he took her hand and placed it ever so gently in his own. I sat looking into the faces of two people whom I had never met, but had longed for all my life, and I was speechless. How would I begin?

"Mr. and Mrs. Jacobs, my name is Sara Jacobs. I am David Jacobs's daughter."

The look on their faces was shock, pain, joy, and disbelief all rolled into one expression. "David Benjamin Jacob's daughter?" they asked.

"Yes."

"How did you find us? It's not very hard to find us, but why did you look for us? What made you think to look for us?" my grandfather asked, bewildered.

"Mr. and Mrs. Jacobs, it was an accident, really," Jonathan chimed in.

"An accident?" my grandmother replied

Jonathan went on. "Well, you see, Mr. and Mrs. Jacobs..."
I interrupted, "I can explain. You see, I was flown here from America to work through the American Embassy as an archaeological/photojournalist at excavation sites here in Jerusalem and surrounding areas. This is my first time in your country. I only looked up

your name to—umm, sorry to say...to pay my respects...visit your graves. I thought you were deceased. I was told you were deceased." There was a silence that seemed like an eternity to me and was broken by the sweet voice of my grandmother. "You did not come here to find us?" she asked.

"Oh, no, it was totally by accident. I had no idea you were alive and living here," I replied.

"How is your father?" my grandfather asked with a painful expression on his face. The lines around his eyes deepened as he waited for my reply.

"He's well."

"What does he do for a living?" he asked.

"He stays busy. He's an investment broker and a part-time professor at a college, teaching international banking."

"This is a miracle of God. Just a miracle! Yeshua has heard our prayers and forgiven us," my grandmother cried.

"I thought you were Orthodox Jews." I said.

My grandparents exchanged glances with the saddest eyes I have ever seen. "Would you like some tea or coffee?" my grandmother asked.

"Thank you. Some water would be nice," I said.

"Thank you, Mrs. Jacobs," Jonathan added.

Before disappearing into the kitchen, my grandmother replied, "Dear, we *used to be* Orthodox Jews."

"Sara, it's a difficult story to tell," my grandfather replied. Trying to hold back the anger rising within me, I remarked, "I'd like to hear the story. I'd like to know why there have been no phone calls, letters—nothing. I'd like to know why my dad has refused to talk with you or about you." I tearfully pleaded, "Why has there been all this secrecy? What could have been so terrible to have no relationship, no communication, and no contact with my dad or his children? Why have you remained hidden from us all these years?"

Jonathan, seeing my obvious distress, took my hand and patted it as if that would slow my racing heart. His eyes told me I needed to calm down and relax. I knew he was right.

My grandmother returned with two glasses of water in fragile looking, hand-blown goblets of fine crystal in a gorgeous blue and gold pattern. I feared that in my nervousness I might drop the glass as she offered it to me. I was still in shock from finding them alive. As I looked around, I imagined my dad sitting in one of the tapestry chairs, drinking from one of these goblets. Oddly enough, it wasn't too difficult to imagine. Now I could better understand my dad's love for elegant tapestries. His taste in fine art was very similar to his father's. Some of the exact paintings in our home adorned the walls of my grandparents' beautiful cottage. I wondered, "How else are my dad and his father alike?"

"If God knew you were here and where I was, why would He keep us apart and you a secret from my brother and me?" I asked nervously.

"You have a brother?" my grandfather asked.

"Yes, you have a grandson. Benjamin Aaron is his name. He's twenty-six years old, two years younger than me," I replied. I took two large gulps of water. "Why would a loving God keep all this hidden from us?" I asked.

My grandmother's voice was soft and soothing. "He didn't, Sara. God's word says that everything hidden will be brought into light. You must not blame God. This isn't God's fault or His doing. If you must blame someone, Sara, then place the blame on us, your grandparents. We made some terrible choices out of fear and anger. We have lived with the choices we made all these years," she said through her tears.

"Would you like to step outside for some air, Sara?" Jonathan asked.

"Yes, please," I agreed.

"Go ahead dear" my grandfather urged.

Ephesians 4:32 "Be kind to one another, tender-hearted, forgiving each other, just as God in Yeshua also has forgiven you."

New American Standard

Colossians 3:12 "So, as those who have been chosen of God, holy and beloved, put on a heart of compassion, kindness, humility, gentleness and patience."

New American Standard

Colossians 3:12-13:"Therefore as God's chosen people, holy and dearly loved, clothe yourselves with feelings of compassion and with kindness, humility, gentleness and patience. Bear with one another; if anyone has a complaint against someone else, forgive him. Indeed, just as the Lord has forgiven you, so you might forgive."

Complete Jewish Bible

CHAPTER 13

Willing to Change

I SAT ON the porch swing looking out across the lawn, feeling angry and hurt. Jonathan followed and sat next to me. "Jonathan, how could my father and mother keep this lie, this secret, all these years? And why?"

"Do you really think it was easy for him? I can't begin to try and give you an answer for what transpired between your dad and his parents. However, I do think you need to give both your dad and your grandparents an opportunity to tell you without judging them beforehand. I can only imagine the pain this secret has caused in the heart of your father all these years."

I was continually amazed at this man sitting next to me. Jonathan had such wisdom and strength. His compassion and fairness on every issue was almost annoying. I had to admit, though, it was a tremendous help to have him with me right now, speaking into my life.

"Can't you put aside the anger for now, and let them explain their story?" Jonathan asked. I nodded yes. "Allow God's grace to cover this situation, Sara. Can you do that?" he asked.

"I will try, Jonathan—I will really try," I told him. Saying that, I had no idea how God's grace covered anything, especially this situation. "I'm not angry at my grandparents or my parents. I'm angry at Jesus, Yeshua," I snapped.

Jonathan chuckled. "Sara, Yeshua gives us a free will to choose and to make right choices. The choices we make often affect and hurt innocent people. We make choices sometimes without ever consulting Yeshua or God or anyone else for advice."

"Jonathan, you seem to be very knowledgeable of the choices that were made here, and extremely understanding. How come?"

"Sara, I had my own choices to deal with and those of others as well. Because of this, hurts and disappointments were caused in my life and the lives of others. I'll share that with you some other time, not now. You have enough to deal with," Jonathan replied. We sat quietly on the porch until I felt ready to return to the house.

When I came back into the living room, my grandparents were sitting together, holding hands. My grandmother had been crying.

"I'm sorry if I've upset you. I hadn't meant to do that. I just wanted to know why my father would tell me that my grandparents are no longer living. I don't even know your full names."

"Abigail Rebecca and Aaron Benjamin Jacobs," Sara I know this has all been very shocking for you to learn you have grandparents. I know it may be too soon, but when you are comfortable please know you can call us Grandmother and Grandfather, but we understand if you cannot do that or choose not to, at least for now, she said softly.

"Now I know where my brother's name came from," I replied. "And my middle name is Rebecca." I ignored the comment regarding what to call them.

"Please sit down, Sara," my grandmother urged. Instead, I walked over to a cherry wood table under an oval mirror and picked up one of the many black-and-white framed photos, of a young man about sixteen years old. "Is this my father?" I asked.

My grandmother came to me and put her hands on my shoulders. "Yes, dear, it is."

I picked up another photo, of an infant. My grandfather walked over to me and also placed his hand on my shoulder. "Sara, we love our son very much. We had his life all planned out from the time he was born. We knew the college he would attend. We knew one day he would marry a sweet Jewish girl and raise a big family and live close to us," he explained.

"He married a sweet gentile girl and they have lived happily for twenty-nine years," I quickly replied.

"We know, Sara, we know," my grandmother responded. "We don't mean to offend you, Sara. We are sure Alana is a wonderful wife and mother. You see, our eyes were closed to anything that was new or different from the way we were raised. We were not open to discuss or even hear anything different from our traditional beliefs and lifestyle. We refused to hear about our son's 'Jesus,'" she added.

"Sara, please try to understand that even our own lives were planned out for us before we were born. Our culture is steeped in tradition and history. Today it is quite different in many Jewish homes. But ours was very strict. My parents adhered to all biblical rules and standards set forth by our rabbi and the Scrolls. This is the way I attempted to set my household. There was much blindness and ignorance in our thinking. My eyes gradually opened, though, and my ears began to listen to God's voice about His son. The only problem was that this began to happen long after our son left. I then began to allow my hurt, rejection, embarrassment, and shame to be healed by the one called Yeshua. Abigail tried to reason with me, but I wouldn't listen. I couldn't get past my own pride and hurt," my grandfather shared.

"What they say is true, Sara," Jonathan added. "I grew up in the same type of household with the same strict teachings they are describing."

My grandfather continued, "I'm sorry to say we did not handle the situation well at all. David begged us to meet Alana, but we refused. We wouldn't even consider it. We were angry, hurt, and disappointed that David had been dishonest with us, but more than that—we were angry that he chose to court someone outside our faith. We demanded he not see Alana again. He was in love with your mother, and he adamantly refused. We gave him a choice, an ultimatum if you will. He could stop seeing Alana and regain his place in our home, hearts, and community, or, if he refused, he could leave our home and our family," Aaron explained.

"How horrible," I thought.

My grandmother, seeing the obvious look on my face, intervened. "Sara, I know this must sound terrible to you, but please try and understand. In our faith, there is no allowance for disrespect or rebellion to parents under any circumstances. There was definitely no allowance for any other form of faith or dedication in our home except to God Jehovah alone. We never believed our son would actually go away. We never believed that he would leave our home, his parents, and his homeland. Nor did we think he would even have the means to run off," she added.

My grandfather replied, "He had friends from school whose parents were moving to the States; that's how he got away. He convinced them to let him go with them and they agreed. Our hearts were broken. I thought his mother would never recover. I was too angry and prideful to stop him. I thought surely he would change his mind, but he didn't. I told him, 'Leave! Never come back! And tell everybody your parents are dead!' It was my fault. I did this." He sat forward in his chair with his face in his hands.

The tears were flowing down both their faces. My coming here had opened old wounds and reawakened the scars left by such a traumatic event. My heart was breaking for them. I held back my own tears. I was like my dad, unable to show my emotions.

Through his tears, my grandfather said, "Sara, I waited and hoped that David would come back. That he would change his mind and apologize. I was so sure he would, but after a few months, I realized how serious he was about his decision, and it made me even angrier. I kept thinking, 'How could he? How could he just leave everything—his parents, his friends, his synagogue, his future, for *this* Jesus?' I had no idea he had left the country. When I tried looking for him here, none of his friends would talk with me. No one ever again spoke to me about David, because they knew how it made me feel."

"So you did try to contact him?" I inquired gently.

"Yes! But it was too late. We let a year go by without ever trying to get in touch with him. We were still hoping and praying he would return to us and beg our forgiveness. Our pain, loss, and embarrassment were too great. My pride was even greater and kept me from making the first move.

"You see, I assumed that David was living somewhere here in the country. I thought that sooner or later we would come together, talk, and work everything out. I never believed the rumors that he had actually left our country. I refused to believe it. We were embarrassed that our friends and rabbi knew of our son's choice and that he dishonored us in this manner. We never considered that we had embarrassed our son by our actions and reactions to something so important in his life," My grandfather cried softly.

"I was thinking more of myself and our reputation," he continued. "I was thinking more about what others thought than what our son was going through. I didn't think about his feelings or hurt. I have many times thought of the pain we—no, *I*, caused him by my foolish pride and stubbornness.

"Sara, the hurt I felt went deep, but my pride went even deeper. God's word says, 'Pride goes before a fall.' Well, I fell all right, into a deep resentment and depression. I was angry with everyone, even God. Abigail tried to stop me from making the decision I did, but I wouldn't listen. I was angry with her for not feeling the same as I did. The difference was that she saw from her heart, not her head. I was too stubborn to listen to her. We honored God and obeyed Him all our lives. Now He was taking my only son from me," he said.

"Sara, I was angry, even bitter with your mother, Alana, for telling our son about Jesus. Little did I know then that He wasn't just *her* Jesus. He was for everyone who would accept Him. Our son had accepted Him," my grandfather added.

My grandmother chimed in, "Sara, our son was our life. We lived for him. He was everything to us." My grandfather nodded in agreement with her.

"Abigail begged me to go to him and make things right, but I refused. When I finally listened to her and my own heart, I decided to go find David, but it was too late. David was already gone. No one knew where he was or how to get in contact with him. I realized too late, Sara that your mother didn't take David from us. God didn't take him, either. It was my pride, my generational beliefs, and stubbornness that caused him to leave. I had to get to a place where my eyes could be opened and I could truly hear from God.

"I prayed day and night before God and read scriptures like I never had before. I fasted and laid myself before God. Unknown to me was that God was softening my heart. He had to work through a lot of pain and anger. He was preparing my heart for something bigger and better than anger or pride. He was preparing me to forgive and to receive forgiveness.

"A few years later, there was someone who thought he knew where David might be in the States. He gave me a phone number. I called the number but the person on the other end of the phone said that David had lived with them a few months, but had moved. They had no address or phone number to give me. I asked them if David ever mentioned his mother Abigail or me. They said no, he never mentioned his parents. They said that David told them his parents were dead. Dead! 'We are not dead!' I shouted in response. I was even angrier after hearing that." My grandfather sighed.

Jonathan broke in. "Sara, for a Jewish father to lose a son in this way is worse than losing him in actual death. There is and always will be a tremendous connection between a Jewish father and son."

"Yes, I can understand. My father and brother are extremely close. Now their relationship makes more sense to me. I often felt left out when they were together. I can understand even more now why my father spent so much time with Benjamin," I told them.

My grandfather spoke again. "I feel in my heart that your father loves you very much. You are a beautiful, wise, and intelligent young woman. You are very much like your father in many ways."

"In what ways?" I asked.

"You are both very bright and caring and a bit stubborn. To search out your roots like this shows great courage and tenacity. Your father certainly has that! You have your father's smile and your mother's beautiful face." My grandfather smiled.

"How do you know what my mother looks like?" I asked. "I thought you refused to meet her."

"Oh I did, but David left some pictures in his desk of the two of them. I could certainly see why he fell so in love," my grandfather replied.

"Aaron, how did you come to accept Yeshua as your Savior?" I asked.

Matthew 6:14 "For if you forgive men when they sin against you, your heavenly Father will also forgive you. But if you do not forgive men their sins, your Father will not forgive your sins."

Complete Jewish Bible

I John 1:9 "If we confess our sins, He is faithful and just and will forgive us our sins and purify us from all unrighteousness."

Open Bible

Acts 3:19 "Repent, then, and turn to God, so that your sins may be wiped out, that times of refreshing may come from the Lord."

Open Bible

CHAPTER 14

Set Up By God

CHANGE DOES NOT come easy. God is a patient and loving God. My grandfather shared his story with us. "It took time, Sara, and a lot of prayer for me to change. It was years later. One day, an Israeli student came to do some work for us. He was studying at the university and looking for a place to stay. We invited him to stay with us until he could find a place of his own. Little did I know this was a plan designed by God to open my eyes and get to know his Son, Yeshua. It was a definite 'setup' by God!

"This young man, whose name was Haviar, was very wise. It seemed he knew just what to say to me, and when to say it. We would sit for hours reading and studying scriptures. He reminded me so much of David. I suppose that is why I was receptive to what he was teaching me. I needed forgiveness, although I didn't know it at the time. I needed to forgive myself most of all. This was a truth Haviar was able to explain to me using the Holy Scriptures. The moment God revealed His Son to me was like no other day I had ever experienced.

"I was finally able to let go of my pride and open my heart to David's Yeshua, who has now become my Yeshua as well. Abigail and I accepted Yeshua, the Messiah, and our lives completely changed. We were like two little children learning to walk again. It took us a while to understand what we needed to know regarding the Messiah and how it all lined up with scripture. Haviar was patient and so kind to us.

God was even more patient and kind. It took us a little time to realize that we didn't have to give up our Jewish heritage, but could add to it.

I finally understood what David had tried to tell me, but I just wouldn't listen. I felt I was betraying my God by listening to him talk about this 'Jesus.' I didn't see how I could be a Jew and follow Yeshua. I was blinded by tradition and I could not see clearly. My ears were closed to hearing about Yeshua. Now, I am free to be who God created me to be, and to serve His Son as well. I only wish it could have been while David was here to witness the transformation in our lives. My heart has ached to see my son and to tell him about our conversion. I have often wondered if he could or would ever forgive me, and if he would ever want me in his life again, even as a believer. What do you think, Sara, would he?" my grandfather asked with tearful eyes.

"I don't know, I couldn't possibly answer that; only my father could," I replied.

My grandfather looked at me with compassion and said, "I have never given up hope of one day seeing my son to beg his forgiveness. I've prayed he will give me another chance to be a part of his life and his children's lives as well.

"Sara, I know I don't deserve anything from him, the way I acted. All I can think is that God is a forgiving God. It's only by grace and mercy that I was changed and can really understand the teachings of Yeshua and who the Messiah is. I would so love to share my transformation with my son." he said.

"My hope is that he would be pleased and happy to know we can share the same faith, and honor the same king. I lost hope for a very long time. Now I sense hope rising again. The only reason this hope is within me now is because you are here. I have prayed every day since I received Yeshua into my heart for help in finding my son. I have prayed that he and I would be reunited. I have hope now that it might happen. I choose to believe that in some way, and with time David will forgive me and come home, at least for a visit. God brought my granddaughter to me. Now I have hope He might bring my son as well," he said.

"I can't say if my father would ever come home again. I have no idea what may happen when he finds out what I've done," I said.

"I understand, Sara, I understand," my grandfather responded. "Our life since David left has been totally different. The friends we had known for years turned against us when we accepted Yeshua. We were no longer welcome in the synagogue, and our rabbi would no longer come to our home or speak with us. I lost everything, I thought. But once I found my life in Yeshua, I couldn't go back. Not a day has gone by that I haven't repented for what I did to our son. Sara, can you forgive your grandparents?" he begged.

The tears were now flowing down my face, too. Jonathan also looked a bit teary eyed as he walked into the kitchen to give us some privacy.

"I don't know what to say. Please give me a little time to digest everything that has been said. This has been a shocking turn of events that I wasn't prepared for. I don't even know how I will tell my dad that I've found you. I don't know if he will be glad, sad, relieved, or angry. I don't know if he will forgive me for uncovering his secret, a secret he has kept hidden in his heart. A secret that he has spent his adult life protecting and keeping from everyone," I replied.

"Sara, we will pray that God will go before you and show you exactly what to say and how to tell your father. We will pray that God will give you His peace. We will pray that our son will hear and feel God's great love as you tell him. We will also pray that our son will open his heart to receive what you share with him and that he will want to be reconciled with us," my grandmother said.

"That's a pretty big prayer, don't you think?" I replied.

"It's not too big for God," my grandfather responded. "Nothing is impossible with God if we only believe. We want to be a part of your lives. We want to meet our grandson, Benjamin."

"What about my mother? Do you want to meet her and be a part of her life too?" I asked.

"Yes, of course we do. We owe her a great apology. We want to ask forgiveness from her as well," my grandfather replied.

"I think I should go now," I said. "This has been a very tiring and stressful day for all of us."

"Will you come back to see us?" my grandmother asked.

"Yes, of course," I agreed.

Jonathan appeared in the doorway and asked if I was ready to leave. I nodded. He spoke in Hebrew to my grandparents as we were leaving. We all shook hands as we said good-bye. I turned to look back as we walked to the car, watching them wave to us. My heart was torn for these two precious parents who had been hurting for so many years. Oh, what a treasure I had uncovered!

Jonathan and I did not talk in the car on the ride back to the hotel. I wondered how or if I should tell my dad about finding his parents. I wondered what the repercussions might be if I did. I couldn't help but wonder if this revelation would destroy my relationship with my own father or damage it at best.

"How can I ever tell my dad I found his parents?" I asked Jonathan. "Don't think about that right now, Sara. You need some rest before you make any decisions about this. You will know what to do when the time comes. You will do it in peace," Jonathan told me.

Exodus 33:14 "My presence will go with you and I will give you rest."

New International Version

Psalm 73:26 "My flesh and my heart may fail, but God is the strength of my heart and my portion forever."

New International Version

Psalm 62:1 "My soul finds rest in God alone.

New King James

CHAPTER 15

Compassion to Forgiveness

I HAD A restless night and got up before sunrise. While showering, I thought of my sweet grandparents. I thought of their pain, guilt, and anguish. I thought of my father's pain, guilt, and anguish. I reflected on my own pain as well. There were so many emotions flooding my mind and heart, I could hardly think.

I considered my own mistakes and how many times I had done things I wished I hadn't, or said something I wished I could take back, but could not. I began to realize it was all because of pride. I remembered the comment Jonathan made accusing me of being prideful. "Oh my goodness," I thought, "I don't want that in my life. I never want to hurt anyone because of my pride."

After I showered and dressed, I got down on my knees and said a childlike prayer asking God for wisdom to say and do the right things today. I really did not want to think of myself as prideful, but if I was, I wanted God to fix it!

I spent the morning on the balcony, coffee cup in hand, watching the beautiful sunrise. I couldn't help wondering what the day would bring. I was still not allowed to go back to work for several more days. This would give me time to really figure out how to approach my dad about his parents.

After a second cup of coffee, I began to reminiscence about the work I had already accomplished here in Israel. I was also musing over the great accolades, honors, and prestige bestowed upon me in the past. I knew my work here would be well received. My pictures would probably be shown in many of the archaeological magazines. Once again, honors would most likely be bestowed upon me. So why didn't I feel excited about it?

My mind wandered back to my grandparents. I wished I could wrap my arms around them and tell them everything would be all right. But I knew I couldn't do that. I had no assurance at this moment that anything would ever be all right again. I kept wondering how in the world I could tell my father about my discovery of his parents. How would he feel about the fact that his daughter had probed into such a personal area of his life?

The phone rang. It was Jonathan. He said he had something to share with me. He said what he had to tell me might bring more clarity to my grandparents' story. We agreed to meet at the hotel's outdoor pool within the next hour. "Wear your swimsuit. The water looks very inviting," he told me.

"Are we going for a swim?" I asked him.

"Why not?" He chuckled.

When I arrived, Jonathan was propped up on a lounge chair, wearing white bathing trunks. His dark sunglasses hung low on his nose. A cocktail waitress was standing over him, taking an order and flirting.

"I was just ordering a drink. What would you like?" he asked me.

"I'll have the same as you, darling," I replied as I stared down the waitress and parked my straw tote bag and towel on the chair next to Jonathan. I then removed my shorts and T-shirt, revealing my stylish black bathing suit that showed off my shapely figure. I decided to dive into the pool and swim a few feet under the water. I floated back up and looked from the edge of the pool at Jonathan.

"So, what's up?" I asked.

Jonathan came over to the pool laughing, and offered me his hand, pulling me up out of the water. "Darling!" he said. "She's not my type," he grinned.

"Come again?" I replied as I toweled down and fell back on the lounge chair.

"The waitress. She's not my type," he told me.

"Good to hear. She's not my type, either," I snipped.

Jonathan chuckled again. Our tropical teas were served, and we clicked glasses as Jonathan gave a toast. "To your new-found treasures!"

"What treasures they were," I thought. We lounged silently, sipping our tea.

Jonathan broke the silence. "Sara, I was raised in the same type of traditional home as your grandparents. Christianity and the name of Yeshua were not allowed in our home. My Jewish friends who first introduced me to Yeshua did so in secret. They knew my parents would object, and they knew I was concerned about my parents finding out. We met together regularly and did extensive and exhausting studies on the prophets in the Old Testament. We compared Old Covenant prophecies to those in the New Covenant.

We went back and forth with revelations of what was prophesied in the Old Testament and how it became truth in the New Testament. The study of Isaiah 53 came alive to me. No one had ever shared these truths, these prophecies with me before. I saw for myself how it all came together to reveal the Messiah, Yeshua. I read in the New Covenant that Yeshua perfectly kept the entire Torah. He taught that He came to fulfill the Torah, not abolish it. Accepting Yeshua as my Messiah did not mean I stopped being Jewish. Messianic Jews do not stop being Jewish; on the contrary, we remain strongly Jewish in identity and lifestyle.

"By the time my parents discovered what I'd been doing, it was too late. I had already accepted Yeshua as my Lord, my Savior. My parents were outraged. They were hurt, disappointed, and embarrassed by their son, just like your grandparents were by your father. My parents felt betrayed by their own son, just as your grandparents felt. I tried to tell them the Tenakh, Old Testament, provides the foundation of our Jewish faith and the New Testament, also written by Jews, is the completion of our Jewish faith. They didn't want to hear anything I had to say."

"Many do not realize that they can have their culture, their traditions, their love and faith in God, and have Yeshua as well. When I tried to explain this to my parents, they said I was talking foolishness. They said it was blasphemy. They told me it was Meshuggina! That means 'crazy' in Hebrew. Their ears, hearts, and minds were closed to anything I had to say on the matter. They gave me a choice, like your father was given. They told me I could end this idiotic talk as they called it or they would send me away. That is how I ended up in Switzerland."

"Tell me more."

"I was in my last year of college and my parents realized I wasn't changing back to their ways or giving up my newfound faith. My father had the resources and connections to get me enrolled in the finest school in Switzerland. That's where I went.

"Couldn't you have just said no?" I asked.

"Yes, I could have said no, Sara, but I wanted to finish my degree, and I knew if I said no, I would not have had a place to live or the financial means to pay for the rest of my schooling. It wasn't what I wanted, but I also thought the time away might be productive for restoring our relationship. I hoped that it might give my parents time to think about all that had happened and maybe they would change their thoughts on the matter."

"Did they at least stay in touch with you?"

"Not the first year. It was very difficult being in a new place, making new friends, having a new faith, and being disconnected from my family."

"What happened? How did it turn out?" I asked.

"It was about three months into the new year when I received a letter from them. It was a letter of apology."

"Apology? Had they accepted Yeshua too?"

"Oh no, nothing like that," he said. "My parents were prideful, stubborn people. Their prestige, their friends, and definitely their synagogue were very high on their list of importance. However, they didn't want to lose their son over a difference of faith. They didn't agree with my choices on my newfound faith, but they wanted us to find some way to stay a family and work through our differences."

"This is what is so powerful about many Jewish people. Some may be headstrong and prideful, but we are faithful to our God and to our families. Family is what God created and we honor and respect that. We work to do whatever is necessary to stay a family. Sometimes we may just have to put our own ideas aside in order to embrace one another. It can be done, and that's what we did."

"I had to make some changes within myself as well. I had to put aside my own resistance, rebellion, and anger toward them. I had to ask God's forgiveness and my parents' forgiveness as well. After all, how could I claim to accept and follow the teachings of Yeshua but not follow what He taught about forgiveness? That would make no sense to anyone," he explained.

Jonathan continued, "My parents were quite impressed with my attitude and drastic change. They asked forgiveness from me and we made peace again. Today they are open to hear my thoughts on scripture, and I can tell God is softening their hearts. I know I must be patient and wait for His timing. One day I am hopeful that they too will accept Yeshua as their Messiah."

"Sara, your grandparents made such great attempts to find your dad. They wanted him to know they had changed. Unfortunately, their wait cost them the physical loss of their son. Your dad, in his own anger and pain, left no door open to be found by his parents. He must have been extremely hurt by his father's actions. Your dad probably felt great rejection from his father. I feel certain that the scars are still fresh, even today," Jonathan explained.

Psalm 37:8 "Refrain from anger, and forsake wrath! Fret not yourself; it tends only to evil."

Psalm 37:8 "Stop being angry, put aside rage, and don't be upset—it leads to evil.

Proverbs 29:22 "A man of wrath stirs up strife, and one given to anger causes much transgression."

Proverbs 19:11 "Good sense makes one slow to anger, and it is his glory to overlook an offense."

Proverbs 14:29 "Being slow to anger goes with great understanding, being quick-tempered makes folly still worse."

CHAPTER 16

God's Restoring Power

"Sara, you must help your dad come to terms with his feelings of anger and rejection toward his parents. He has missed out on so much by his own choices. You can't change him or make him want to see his parents, but you can pray for him. God can move on his heart and work within him for change. You may be delighted at finding grandparents you never knew you had, but he's known all along he had parents living here. He still did not reach out to them," Jonathan said.

"Your dad has no idea how long his parents searched for him or what they were experiencing during his time of silence. He doesn't know how they've changed, or how much they love him. Sara, maybe your father has just been waiting to find his way home and you are the one to help him. Maybe you are the key to turn the lock of his heart," he told me.

"Oh, Jonathan, is that really possible?" I asked.

"Of course it is. Anything is possible with God," Jonathan replied.

"I wish I could believe that. Really I do, Jonathan."

"Sara, God has a much bigger plan and purpose for your trip here than all your wonderful photographs and archaeological projects. I believe He used your expertise and talents to give you favor with our government and embassy. He wanted to get you to a place where you could be effective in having your prayers answered and your dreams fulfilled. I believe His plan was to have you find the grandparents you always hoped and longed for. Now it's up to you as to what you do with what he has revealed to you," Jonathan insisted. "Would you like for me to pray for you, Sara?" he asked.

"Yes, please, and thank you."

Right there at the pool, Jonathan took my hand and softly began to pray, first in Hebrew, then in English. His words were powerful. I knew God heard them. I hoped one day I could pray like Jonathan prayed. I didn't want to merely say sweet words to God. I wanted to pray with meaning, with words that spoke to the problem, with words that had power behind them. I had never heard that kind of prayer before. I felt something inside when he finished praying. Now I understood the faith my mom had told me about all those years. It was only at that moment that I experienced it for myself. I felt refreshed. I felt peaceful and almost giddy. Jonathan and I glanced at one another with silly grins and headed for the pool.

I screamed and laughed as I splashed in the water. I felt such a release of tension. I was swimming like a mermaid underwater when Jonathan jumped in to pull me up to the surface. We floated to the top with his arms around me, both of us giggling and laughing.

That evening Jonathan took me to a wonderful restaurant by the sea. We walked along the seashore after dinner as the sun was setting. Jonathan reached for my hand. When I placed my hand in his, I felt an immediate comfort and safety that I'd never felt before. Warmth began to flow over my body and my heart began to pound strongly. I was afraid Jonathan might even hear it. I had experienced so many beautiful sunsets here, but tonight it meant so much more, having Jonathan beside me. We basked together in a comfortable silence, a language without words.

All too quickly we were back at my hotel. Jonathan walked me to my door and gently kissed me good night. He smiled and winked at me. "See you in the morning, my princess of the Nile." I felt like a high school kid on her first date and it was wonderful. I had never had this particular feeling before, and I liked it.

Before retiring to bed, I called my grandparents and told them I would call my dad soon. I just wasn't sure how long "soon" would be. I needed more time to digest everything. They asked how I was holding up. "Fine, I'm doing just fine. Don't worry about me. I'm fine," I told them. Yet, I knew I wasn't fine, and they probably knew that as well.

"Sara, please come and see us tomorrow," my grandfather pleaded.

"Yes, of course I will. I really want you both to be a part of my life and my family's lives. Finding the two of you was a dream come true." I sighed. "And yes, to the question you asked me."

"What question, Sara?" my grandfather asked.

"You asked if I would forgive you. I'm sorry I didn't tell you then, but I had to know I was answering from my heart. Yes, yes, I forgive you," I said, almost in tears.

"That's wonderful, Sara. I am so happy. You have made Abigail and me so happy," he told me.

"I'm really happy too. Good night, Grandfather, and please tell Grandmother good night for me," I replied.

"There was a pause, and I could hear Aaron clearing his throat. "Good night, my sweet granddaughter, and sleep well," he said.

Over the next few weeks, I spent much time with my grandparents. I wanted to learn about their life together, about my dad growing up. I wanted my grandmother to teach me how to make some of her Jewish dishes. Every time I entered their home I could smell the fresh baked Mandel Bread which is actually a crunchy cookie. She made the best Rugelach which is a cookie made with butter, cream cheese, flour sugar, raisins, walnuts, and cinnamon, and is so delicious! I had tasted these treats at the Marzipan Bakery in Jerusalem and had the most amazing chocolate rugelach, but I do think my grandmother's cookies were even better!

She showed me how to make Matzo Ball Soup. This is delicious little carbohydrate balls drenched in chicken soup. Of course my grandmother added vegetables of carrots, onions and celery and some of Israel's finest spices. The aroma of fresh market vegetables mixed with these delicious spices was like nothing I had ever smelled and I knew I would never forget. The aroma filled the house tantalizing our taste buds!

We laughed a great deal because my grandmother soon witnessed how little I knew about cooking. She quickly figured out that I had spent little time in the kitchen! My mother had attempted many times to show me how to make some of these same dishes, but I just didn't have the patience or interest at the time. One dish I wanted to surprise my mother with was the Borekas. These are heavenly little parcels of dough, crisped with hot oil or melted butter and filled with any desired filling such as potato, spinach or cheese. These fried pastry pouches are nothing short of edible perfection.

And for Shabbat dinner one evening I made potato kugel. It's like a giant tater tot, but I used sweet potato and added cinnamon and sugar so it was like eating a super dessert during the main course.

My mother would be so surprised and hopefully proud that I had learned to cook a few Jewish dishes. My grandfather came in the kitchen "sniffing" one Friday before Shabbat asking who was making Cholent. It's a delicious meat dish made with chicken, lamb, beans, potatoes, onions, paprika, salt, black pepper, turmeric, and garlic, yum!! It was slow cooked all day and the aroma was divine. We could hardly wait until it was time to eat! My grandfather, of course, raved on and on about what a wonderful cook I was becoming and how delicious this cholent tasted. He bragged on everything I made.

I was feeling such love, warmth and joy from my grandparents. They were so amazing to me and knowledgeable about so many things. No matter what I asked, they seemed to have the answer and I ask lots of questions. They showed me many pictures of my dad growing up and as a young man. He was very handsome then and still is today. He does resemble both his parents in different ways.

I shared with my grandparents our life growing up and the way our dad had trained us in the Jewish beliefs and traditions. This seemed to make my grandparents very happy. They were quite blessed when I lit the candles and said the prayers at Shabbat. Tears filled both their eyes and joy was evident on their faces.

We spent time in the Bible sharing and reading scripture. They prayed over me each time I was with them and always before I left to go back to my hotel. Jonathan came with me several times to visit them. They liked Jonathan and he liked them. Jonathan and my grandfather enjoyed talking about scripture. They talked and laughed a lot when they were together.

I knew God was restoring my grandparents not only spiritually, but emotionally as well. I watched the lines around my grandfather's eyes fade and the sadness in his eyes began to disappear. I observed his stature changing from one with shoulders rounded from the heaviness of the load he had carried, to standing straight and erect. There was a sparkle of life and a glimmer of hope in him that he might get to see his son once again.

I saw my grandmother's smile broaden with every mention of my dad. I heard her laugh out loud, which was something I had not heard since I'd, met her. I watched the two of them smiling at one another and embracing warmly from time to time. They reminded me of little children waiting for some special present to arrive. I could only pray that God would fulfill their greatest desire and hope. Their desire was to see their only son again. I was so afraid and concerned that it might not happen. How could they possibly bear more pain if he didn't want to come home? I couldn't help wonder if my being here, as wonderful as it was for me, would result in more wounds, more hurt for them. I pushed those thoughts out of my head as I listened to the two of them talking so happily together. I tried to believe for the best, as difficult as that was for me.

I witnessed God move in ways I had only been told about as a child. For the first time in my adult life, I found myself talking to

God. I prayed to God and I began trusting Him in ways I never thought I could on my own. I knew my heart was being changed every time I sat with my grandparents and listened to their stories. I could see a picture of God's hand gently pulling back each layer of their hearts, as a masterful engraver would do. I felt He was placing all the hurt, brokenness, and rejection on His potter's wheel with precise timing like that of a well-trained potter. I knew in my heart He was restoring what no one could do in the natural world. His mercy and grace was overwhelming me.

Psalms 34:18 "Adonai is near those with broken hearts; he saves those whose spirit is crushed."

Complete Jewish Bible

Psalms 34:18 "The Lord is close to the brokenhearted and saves those who are crushed in spirit."

New International Version

CHAPTER 17

Change of Heart

THE RAINS HAD continued longer than expected. My time off had been extended into several weeks. But the rainy season would soon be over and my work would resume. I was extremely grateful for the time I'd been able to spend with my grandparents. The time off offered me a chance to prepare myself for the call to my dad. I knew I couldn't put it off any longer.

One early evening, I called my parents' house. When I heard my dad's voice, fear gripped me, and I almost hung up. Once again my mind raced with questions of what to say, or not say. Is this the right time? Will he understand? Will he forgive me? The sound in my head was a roar I felt could be heard on the streets. I shook my head slightly as if that would relieve all the nagging questions.

"Hello, Dad. It's Sara."

"Sara, how good to hear from you! We haven't heard from you in a while. Are you all right?"

"Yes, Dad, I'm fine. How is Mom? Is she there?"

"Yes, she is right here. Do you want to speak with her?"

"In a moment, Dad, in a moment," I told him. I struggled for the right words to say. Nothing came to mind at first. Then suddenly I remembered Jonathan's encouragement to me. He had told me, "God will be with you like he was with Moses. Just open your mouth and God will fill it." Oh, I hoped he was right. Then I began.

"Dad, I need to tell you something."

"Yes, Sara, what is it? Is anything wrong?"

"Please don't be angry with me."

"Angry with you, Sara? Why would I be angry with you?"

"Dad, I decided to try and find your parents' grave sites and pay my respects to them while I was here. Instead, I discovered that they aren't dead at all, but very much alive and living right here in Jerusalem. But then you knew that already, didn't you? I've been spending time getting to know them these past few weeks. Dad, why did you tell Benjamin and me they were dead? I don't understand."

In my rush of conversation I realized I'd hardly taken a breath or given my dad any time to respond. There was a long pause of silence on the other end of the line. I could hear my mother in the background and I just knew she was praying. "Dad, are you there?" Still there was no answer. "Dad, are you there?" I asked again. Finally, and with a totally different sound in his voice, he responded.

"Yes, Sara, I'm here. Sara, I really don't want to talk about this now."

Anger was rising within me and I was furiously working to push it down. I knew my father could hear my voice change. Not realizing it, I began to speak in a louder tone. "I think I have the right to know now why you would lie to Benjamin and me all these years. How could you keep this from me when you knew I was coming here? Why didn't you just tell me the truth?" I pleaded.

"I guess I just didn't know how," he said. "It had been so long, and I had pushed my parents so far into the past that I didn't know how to bring them into the present. I had no idea you would go looking for them. I think about your grandparents every day, Sara. I always wished I could go back and undo what has been done by me. I reacted in such a hasty, immature, and hateful way. I let my pride hinder me, convincing myself I was right and they were wrong. The truth was that we were both wrong. Neither of us would lay our pride aside long enough to listen to one another."

My dad continued talking, his voice cracking. "The hurt increased and the anger mounted, Sara. The only answer clear to me at the time was to disappear. I decided I would build my own family and move forward. However, the hurt and pain of losing my parents the way I did never left me. The guilt of keeping them from my children was ever present. I never seemed to be able to follow through with a phone call, although I attempted many times. I was still afraid of rejection. I was afraid my anger would get in the way if I did talk with them. I had no idea if they had changed, or if they even wanted to hear from me. I am sorry I lied to you and Benjamin," he said, between the gasp of tears.

"Please don't cry. Dad, I'm sorry," I begged.

"I just didn't know how else to handle the situation, Sara. When you come home I will explain exactly what happened. Maybe then you can understand. Pretending my parents were gone, dead, seemed the easiest way out. It has turned out to be the hardest thing I've ever dealt with in my life. I knew the way I handled things with my parents was wrong. I was alone, young, and very much in love. I didn't think too clearly about the future at that moment," he said.

"There was no one to counsel me to do differently. I was afraid to ask anyone's opinion in fear of the answer I would receive. Perhaps now you can understand a little better why I became upset with you when you asked questions about my parents. It brought back all the pain and guilt I'd tried so hard to hide. Sara, can you, will you forgive me?" he asked.

Tears were streaming down my face. "Dad, do you remember the Bible stories you and Mom read to me and Benjamin when we were children?" I asked him. "They were stories that talked about God's love and forgiveness."

"Yes, Sara, I remember."

"Well, Dad, I did listen and I do remember them. The one part that always stuck out for me was when it said unless we forgive, God can't forgive us."

"Yes, Sara, that's correct."

"Dad, I do forgive you, and I love you. I just wish it hadn't taken so long for this to happen. Dad, God says there is a time for everything under the sun. I guess this is that time."

"Sara, how in the world did you find them? What did they say to you when you did?" he asked.

"Oh, Dad, I have so much to tell you. I will share the whole story with you. It's definitely a 'God thing.' As you know, I had no idea they were alive and living here, but God certainly did! My grandparents are so nice. They were so happy to meet me. Dad, they had so much to tell me, so much you need to hear. They tried to find you, but it was too late. You had already left the country. Dad, I believe they are different than you remember them. They have missed you so much. They want to see you."

"Sara, do you really believe my parents want to see me?" he asked softly.

"Oh yes, Dad," I said. "I know they do, more than anything in the whole world. They want to meet Mom and Benjamin too. They have so much love to express to you, and quite a surprise for you."

"A surprise? Sara, what kind of surprise?"

"It's something that they must share with you in person. No one can share their surprise like they can. Dad, they love you so much. They have been so sad all these years. They are not the parents you remember. Will you give them the opportunity to tell you themselves? Will you let them meet Benjamin? They really are wonderful people, Dad. I know Benjamin would love them as much as I do. They are so easy to love.

"Will you come and meet them, Dad? You, Mom, and Benjamin?" I pleaded.

"Sara, that's a big request, and one I don't know that I can fill. It's been a long time and a lot of years have passed between us. I wouldn't even know how to approach them," he told me.

"I'll be here with you, Dad. Your parents will make it easy for you, I promise. Please say you will come. Do this for me and for Benjamin. No, Dad, do this for you. You and your parents need this time together."

"Let me think about it, Sara. I'll really have to pray about this. I'll call you tomorrow," he told me.

"Thanks, Dad. I love you, and God loves you even more." I was shocked at my own words, but I knew they were true.

It took me a while to get to sleep. The conversation with my dad kept replaying in my head. I knew this was definitely a time for prayer. As best I could, I petitioned God for help. I was excited, yet somewhat nervous about my dad's decision. What if he didn't want to return home? What if his fear kept him from seeing his parents? What if he really *was* angry with me for finding his parents? I drifted off to sleep with those thoughts racing through my mind.

The next morning came with hope and a tinge of fear as well. The "what ifs" from the night before continued to replay in my mind. I kept pushing them away, but slowly they would creep back. I knew I needed to trust God and be at peace, but it was so hard for me. This trust stuff, and waiting on God, was all new to me.

I remembered the prayers my grandparents prayed for me each time we were together. They said powerful prayers, full of hope and faith and assurance of God's love and power. They talked with me about the power of agreement and how God is a God of love and restoration. Oh, how I wanted to believe them!!

My grandparents were the most amazing people and I was so happy and content every time we were together. I knew they felt the same way. They always seemed to know what to say to soothe my fears and concerns and I knew that was the way grandparents were supposed to be. I had missed out on a great deal growing up without them, but I was determined to enjoy the time we had together now and looked forward to our times together in the future. My prayer was that my dad could enjoy it with us.

Jonathan's prayers were just as powerful. I remember the day he prayed for me sitting by the pool. I had never had anyone pray over me like that. My mother was an amazing prayer warrior and I was sure she had been fervently praying since my phone call home. My dad always said strong prayers of faith, but there was just something about the way Jonathan prayed that I really believed what he was praying. He encouraged me every time we were together. He spoke words of strength to me just when I felt weak and always said something to bring me joy.

I knew God was changing me, changing my attitude, my prayer life and my heart, and I really wasn't giving Him much help in the matter. Yet, He seemed to be doing just fine without my input. Jonathan kept telling me, "All God wants is your faith to believe." That sounded so simple and easy, but oh so hard for me when I did try to believe. I fervently prayed, not about what I wanted, but what God wanted in all this and I knew I had to trust Him in His plan and purpose for each of us.

I had so much to learn about faith and waiting. I remember Jonathan telling me one scripture that kept ringing in my thoughts that said, "Be still and know that I am God". It was really difficult for me to be still or be quiet! Jonathan had learned that about me early on, but it hadn't seemed to bother him, at least not that I could tell. I hope it didn't bother God!

Matthew 18:19 "Again, truly I tell you that if two of you on earth agree about anything they ask for, it will be done for them by my Father in heaven".

Complete Jewish Bible

"Intoxicated with unbroken success, we have become too self sufficient to feel the necessity of redeeming and preserving grace, too proud to pray to the God that made us."

Abraham Lincoln

CHAPTER 18

God's Amazing Grace

JONATHAN WAS WAITING down in the lobby, as usual, to take me for brunch. "Boy, do you look happy. Have you uncovered another hidden treasure? Your smile says you have something new to tell me," Jonathan said with a chuckle.

"Yes, I have something wonderful to tell you!" I never imagined the impact this secret discovery could have on my family. I wasn't sure whether to keep this treasure buried or unearth the amazing contents for all of my family to know. "Last night I made a decision. Let me tell you what happened," I told him.

"Dr. Jacobs, a phone call for you, long distance from the States," the desk clerk replied.

"Yes, I'll take it. Excuse me, Jonathan. I'll be right back." It was my dad on the other end of the line.

"Sara, I've been praying for most of the night. We're making plans now to come to Jerusalem."

"All three of you, Dad? Is Benjamin coming too?" I asked.

"Yes, Sara, Benjamin is coming too," he told me.

Tears ran down my face. I could hardly contain my joy. "Thanks, Dad. Thank you so much. We'll be waiting for you. You won't regret it."

"I hope you are right, Sara. I really do. I must tell you, this wasn't an easy decision, but one I feel I needed to make," Dad replied. "It's good to know that I will soon be on my way home. We will be in touch to let you know our travel arrangements," he told me.

"I can hardly wait, Dad, I can hardly wait," I said to him.

Jonathan was anxiously waiting to know what happened. I ran toward him full of excitement, and without thinking about it, put my arms around him. "My family is coming to Jerusalem! My father is coming home," I told him. Jonathan held onto me in a warm embrace.

We raced over to my grandparents' home to give them the fantastic news. The door opened, and there stood my grandfather, anticipation on his face. I hugged him with the tightest hug I could give him, as I had so often dreamed of doing, and said, "Grandfather, your son is coming home!"

He cried and shouted and praised God. He called my grandmother to come quickly to share the good news. I looked into the eyes of my father's mother, as I held out my arms for an embrace. She smiled and hugged me tightly. "Grandmother, your prayers have been answered," I whispered in her ear.

God's grace was overwhelming me. His love was overpowering. The future for all of us looked brighter than any of us thought possible. This archaeological assignment had unearthed the greatest treasure I could ever have discovered.

My grandparents were such beautiful treasures. Treasures hidden so deep that it took time to unearth them. The beauty and fragility of this treasure could not be seen in any photograph, in any book. It was a treasure of the heart. A treasure kept by God's hand. He allowed me to discover this hidden treasure in His time and in His way. God had the perfect key to open this locked box of secrets. I had no idea His plan was to use me to find this amazing treasure. He had me to unearth it, gently unveil its contents, and find a way to bring beauty to the ashes of pain, guilt, hurt, and remorse within this box. God surely does give us beauty for ashes and joy for mourning. What an amazing find this had been!

I found grandparents I never knew I had. My family was going to be restored. I had developed a relationship with God I didn't know was possible. I also met the most wonderful man, Jonathan, who changed my life and my heart in ways I never could have imagined.

The door closed behind us with cries and shouts of joy echoing throughout the house. Plans were already being made for the homecoming for a son thought to have been lost forever. We continued to hug one another and give thanks to God. We knew this was just the beginning of the many blessings God had in store! Praise Adonai!!

Hebrews 4:16 "Let us then with confidence draw near to the throne of grace that we may receive mercy and find grace to help in time of need."

New American Standard

John 1:14 "And the Word became flesh and dwelt among us, and we have seen His glory, glory as of the only Son from the Father, full of grace and truth."

New American Standard

John 14:6 Yeshua (Jesus) said to him, "I am the way, and the truth, and the life. No one comes to the Father except through me."

Complete Jewish Bible

Acts 4:12 "There is salvation in no one else! For there is no other name under heaven given to mankind by whom we must be saved

Complete Jewish Bible

"Grace --it is sovereign, it is free, it is sure, it is unconditional, and it is everlasting."

Alexander Whyte

Made in the USA
Columbia, SC
12 May 2019